Elizabeth Ferrars and The Murder Room

》》 This title is part of The Murder Room, our series dedicated to making available out-of-print or hard-to-find titles by classic crime writers.

Crime fiction has always held up a mirror to society. The Victorians were fascinated by sensational murder and the emerging science of detection; now we are obsessed with the forensic detail of violent death. And no other genre has so captivated and enthralled readers.

Vast troves of classic crime writing have for a long time been unavailable to all but the most dedicated frequenters of second-hand bookshops. The advent of digital publishing means that we are now able to bring you the backlists of a huge range of titles by classic and contemporary crime writers, some of which have been out of print for decades.

From the genteel amateur private eyes of the Golden Age and the femmes fatales of pulp fiction, to the morally ambiguous hard-boiled detectives of mid twentieth-century America and their descendants who walk our twenty-first century streets, The Murder Room has it all. **》》**

The Murder Room
Where Criminal Minds Meet

themurderroom.com

Elizabeth Ferrars (1907–1995)

One of the most distinguished crime writers of her generation, Elizabeth Ferrars was born Morna Doris MacTaggart in Rangoon and came to Britain at the age of six. She was a pupil at Bedales school between 1918 and 1924, studied journalism at London University and published her first crime novel, *Give a Corpse a Bad Name*, in 1940, the year that she met her second husband, academic Robert Brown. Highly praised by critics, her brand of intelligent, gripping mysteries was also beloved by readers. She wrote over seventy novels and was also published (as E. X. Ferrars) in the States, where she was equally popular. *Ellery Queen Mystery Magazine* described her as 'the writer who may be the closest of all to Christie in style, plotting and general milieu', and the *Washington Post* called her 'a consummate professional in clever plotting, characterization and atmosphere'. She was a founding member of the Crime Writers Association, who, in the early 1980s, gave her a lifetime achievement award.

By Elizabeth Ferrars
(published in The Murder Room)

Toby Dyke
Murder of a Suicide (1941)
  aka *Death in Botanist's Bay*

Police Chief Raposo
Skeleton Staff (1969)
Witness Before the Fact (1979)

Superintendent Ditteridge
A Stranger and Afraid (1971)
Breath of Suspicion (1972)
Alive and Dead (1974)

Virginia Freer
Last Will and Testament (1978)
Frog in the Throat (1980)
I Met Murder (1985)
Beware of the Dog (1992)

Andrew Basnett
The Crime and the Crystal (1985)
The Other Devil's Name (1986)
A Murder Too Many (1988)
A Hobby of Murder (1994)
A Choice of Evils (1995)

Other novels
The Clock That Wouldn't
  Stop (1952)

Murder in Time (1953)
The Lying Voices (1954)
Enough to Kill a Horse (1955)
Murder Moves In (1956)
  aka *Kill or Cure*
We Haven't Seen Her Lately
  (1956)
  aka *Always Say Die*
Furnished for Murder (1957)
Unreasonable Doubt (1958)
  aka *Count the Cost*
Fear the Light (1960)
The Sleeping Dogs (1960)
The Doubly Dead (1963)
A Legal Fiction (1964)
  aka *The Decayed Gentlewoman*
Ninth Life (1965)
No Peace for the Wicked (1966)
The Swaying Pillars (1968)
Hanged Man's House (1974)
The Cup and the Lip (1975)
Experiment with Death (1981)
Skeleton in Search of a
  Cupboard (1982)
Seeing is Believing (1994)
A Thief in the Night (1995)

The Crime and the Crystal

Elizabeth Ferrars

An Orion book

Copyright © Peter MacTaggart 1985

The right of Elizabeth Ferrars to be identified as the author of this work has
been asserted in accordance with the Copyright, Designs and Patents Act 1988.

This edition published by
The Orion Publishing Group Ltd
Orion House
5 Upper St Martin's Lane
London WC2H 9EA

An Hachette UK company
A CIP catalogue record for this book is available from the British Library

ISBN 978 1 4719 0684 8

www.orionbooks.co.uk

CHAPTER 1

‘"The way was long, the wind was cold,
The Minstrel was infirm and old . . ."'

The way ahead was certainly going to be very long and the
December evening was very cold, and although Andrew
Basnett was not a minstrel, but a retired professor of botany
from one of London University's many colleges, the thought
of the journey on which he was embarking made him feel
very old and infirm indeed. Seventy-one, after all, was an
advanced age at which to be setting out to go half way round
the world.

He did not always feel that he was very old. Sometimes
he felt hardly more than middle-aged. But the business
of carrying a suitcase which had somehow become noticeably heavier than it would have felt a few years ago,
and of making sure that he had not mislaid any of his hand
luggage, or the book that he meant to read on the plane,
and of trying to convince himself that his ticket and his passport were safe in the pocket where they ought to be, was
just the sort of thing that brought on the sense of help-
lessness that made him feel every one of his seventy-one
years.

‘"Pibroch of Donuil Dhu,
Pibroch of Donuil,
Wake thy wild voice anew,
Summon Clan Conuil . . ."'

For several days Andrew's mind had been hopelessly
under the spell of Walter Scott. Not that he admired Scott's

1

versification in the least. Some of the novels he could just take, but nearly all the verse, he thought, was regrettable. Yet it had a compulsive rhythm to it which, once it started in his brain, repeated itself over and over again until he grew really angry with himself for being unable to become absorbed in something more inspiring, a Shakespeare sonnet, perhaps, or some Milton or Donne.

The trouble was that as a child he had relished Scott intensely. Also, up to the age of twelve or so he had had a habit of automatically memorizing everything he read that had a strong rhythm, particularly if it was related to blood, treachery and terror, and all that he had read thus had remained indelibly printed on his brain for life. His interest in violence had been strange, because he had been a fairly quiet child, not in the least addicted to quarrelling and fighting. But perhaps that had been the trouble. A more ferocious child might later have acquired a taste for more delicate lyrics and gentler fantasy.

Nowadays, of course, when he became subject to the unceasing repetition of some verse, Andrew knew that there was a simple reason for it. It was merely that it helped to blot out something else that he did not want to think about. Something was upsetting him, or scaring him, or making demands on him that he did not know how to meet. And at the moment, as he sat in the departure lounge of Terminal Three at Heathrow, it was naturally the journey ahead of him that was intimidating him, driving him to quote stanza after stanza of Scott to himself.

> '"Come away, come away,
> Hark to the summons!
> Come in your war array,
> Gentles and commons . . .
>
> Leave untended the herd,
> The flock without shelter,

2

> Leave the corpse uninterred,
> The bride at the altar . . .""'

What a deplorable character this Donuil Dhu must have been, he reflected, interfering in other people's private lives to the extent suggested by those lines. Yet he had been muttering them to himself for days, sometimes actually aloud, because after all there was usually no one to overhear him now. Since the death of his wife, Nell, of cancer over ten years ago, he had got more and more into the habit of talking aloud to himself when he was alone in his flat, a pleasant flat in St John's Wood, which all of a sudden he now thought himself insane to be leaving, even for the two months that he had planned.

What was this urge, he wondered, that from time to time drove one out from one's comfortable home, where one enjoyed all the pleasures of privacy, of being able to lay one's hand immediately on anything that one wanted, of having the books around one that one was likely to want to read, of being able to reach most of one's friends, when privacy became boring or depressing, simply by lifting the telephone? The thought of travel, considered several months ahead, might seem immensely attractive, but when the time of departure came near Andrew nearly always found himself wishing desperately that he had not been such a fool as to commit himself to it.

However, when the crowd in the departure lounge began to move, surging slowly into the belly of a great jumbo jet, his spirits began to rise. He had always found waiting difficult. It was not exactly that he was an impatient man, but he was inclined to believe, if he was compelled against his will to do nothing for a time, that someone was maliciously and deliberately inflicting delay on him. Yet whenever he was setting out on a journey he always arrived far earlier than was necessary, thus wilfully imposing on himself that irritating waiting. This evening he had arrived at Heathrow more than an hour before the time for checking in and so was feeling moderately tired even before the journey started.

But action was a restorative. As he made his way to the seat that had been assigned to him a flicker of excitement banished unwanted verses from his mind and left him wondering how soon he would be able to get a drink.

He had not very long to wait, for once the plane had penetrated the cloud cover and it was permitted to undo seat-belts, a trolley came round from which Andrew obtained the whisky which his system was craving. Then there came a meal of sorts and after that a film was shown on a screen at the front of the cabin. But as he had not accepted the earphones that had been offered to him, the faces that he saw were merely strangely mouthing things, almost funny, like characters in an old silent comedy, though he deduced from the number of guns that appeared, the use of which seemed to dispose effectively of a fair number of people, and the cars that crashed into each other, that it was probably a very bloodthirsty thriller that he was watching.

He had intended to start reading as soon as the meal was over, yet he found that he could not stop watching the incomprehensible film and by the time that it ended he was too tired to begin on his book. He knew that he would not sleep. He never could sleep on a plane. But he could not do anything else either because he always found himself so abominably uncomfortable. Though he was a spare man who did not find it difficult to adjust himself to the narrowness of the seats, he was tall and had long legs and there was never anywhere to put them.

All the same, as the hours slowly passed, as daylight succeeded darkness, then darkness came again, he dozed occasionally, rousing himself at intervals to eat some of the incredibly dreadful food with which he was presented. Breakfast was the worst, if it really was breakfast. He had lost count of time. Was it night or day? Was this breakfast or a peculiar kind of supper? He was not at all sure and he was not sure either what day of the week it was. He knew that the journey took approximately twenty-four hours, yet according to the calendar it took two days, which was really very confusing.

The breakfast that he found so abominable consisted of an omelet made unmistakably of powdered egg, a sausage encased in a tough jacket of plastic, and a roll that had seen better days. During the war and the years of austerity that had followed it Andrew had often enough been grateful for omelets made of powdered egg, but it had not occurred to him for a long time now that he would ever have to face such a thing again. To be offered it on this flight, which after all was fairly expensive, struck him as positively an insult. He left the meal nearly untouched, only drinking the cup of pallid coffee that went with it.

After that he started hankering for whisky again, but a puritanical sense that if this was really breakfast there would be a certain impropriety in following it immediately with alcohol checked his impulse to go and see if he could get some at the bar. His digestion assured him that the time was about nine o'clock in the evening, but there was daylight outside the windows again and he was afraid that the meal really had been breakfast.

A long time ago, as it now seemed, the plane had landed at Muskat and then at Singapore, and now it was on the last stage of its journey. Only a little while after the breakfast had been cleared away the sign commanding the fastening of seat-belts was illuminated and soon afterwards the plane bumped on the ground and taxied to a standstill. Andrew stood up, yawning, stretching the joints that had stiffened during the night or day or whatever it had been, plucked his hand luggage and overcoat from the locker over his head and joined the throng making its way towards the exit.

Once in the airport he found that he was required to put

his hand luggage on a bench, and to stand a little way back from it while a large and beautiful Alsatian was led up to sniff it. Andrew's first thought was that the dog had been trained to sniff for high explosive and that if this were so, standing back about six feet from the bench would not be much protection. But then his mind, addled though it was by fatigue, cleared somewhat and he realized that what the dog was sniffing for was drugs. Cannabis, or perhaps even heroin. He looked at the handsome animal with sympathy. He had read somewhere that the dogs that were trained to perform this service often became addicts themselves and did not take long to die.

Today the dog showed no interest in Andrew's luggage or in that of anyone who followed him and he was allowed to pick up his bag, go through passport control, collect his suitcase beyond it, and then found himself mercifully waved through Customs without having to open anything. With relief that the journey was over, he stepped out of the air-conditioned shade of the airport into Adelaide's heat and golden glare of sunshine.

'Andrew!'

He had been expecting it, yet had had an unreasonable fear that something would go wrong with the arrangements that had been made for meeting him. He had had an uncomfortable feeling that he would have to find a taxi for himself, if such a thing should actually be available at the airport, and have himself driven to the address that he had noted down, perhaps only to find that there was no one at home and that he would have to plant himself, exhausted, in the doorway and wait there for he did not know how long.

Absurd, because Tony Gardiner was not a man to let anyone down, especially since it had been his own idea that he should meet Andrew's plane, though it was due to arrive at what, according to the Australian clock, was an appallingly early hour.

Tony, whom Andrew had not seen for four years, was thirty-five now, though he had always looked younger than he was because of the way his fair, curly hair sprang up from his forehead, the candour of his clear blue eyes, the friendly curve of his mouth and the healthy tan of his skin. He was about six foot tall, wide-shouldered and strongly built. This morning he was wearing shorts, a dark blue, open-necked shirt and sandals on his bare feet. Emerging from the crowd of people who were waiting behind a barrier to meet friends and relations who had arrived on the plane, he gripped Andrew's hand and shook it vigorously. Then, while Andrew was still blinking in the sunlight, Tony picked up his luggage with the effortlessness of relative youth and suggested to Andrew that he should take off his overcoat, which he had just put on because that was the easiest way of carrying it, assuring him that he would soon find the morning intolerably hot.

Leading the way to his car, Tony went on, 'What sort of journey did you have? Everything all right?'

'Well, it was pretty horrible, of course,' Andrew replied, 'but there's something to be said for getting it over quickly instead of breaking it, and then sleeping it off as soon as you can.'

They got into the car.

'That's right,' Tony said. 'You can sleep now as long as you like. Jan's sorry she isn't here to meet you, but she's had to go to work.'

Jan was the wife whom Tony had acquired a few months ago. Andrew had never met her and knew very little about her. At the time, four years ago, when on retiring he had made his first trip round the world, breaking the journey often to lecture in New Zealand, Australia and India, Tony had still been unmarried. He had also been living in Canberra, where he had not yet begun to specialize in marine carbohydrates, as he did at present, having only recently moved to Adelaide to a job in the Institute of Marine Biology in the suburb of Betty Hill.

His friendship with Andrew was of long standing. It had begun about twelve years before when Tony had spent three years in England, working for a Ph.D. in the department of which Andrew had been professor. In his occasional letters since that time he had always pressed him to make a second visit to Australia, not to lecture but simply as a guest who would be welcomed by old friends and would avoid the dreariness of an English winter. At first Andrew had not considered the suggestion seriously, but then an unexpected legacy had made him suddenly feel far richer than usual and had made him decide to accept the invitation. And at last, with the journey behind him, he was beginning to feel very glad that he had done so.

'Of course, I never believed you'd really come,' Tony said. 'We've been talking about it for so long, haven't we? Even a week ago Jan and I said you might call it off at the last minute.'

'No, there was no risk of that,' Andrew said. 'I've been saying to myself it's now or never, and I certainly didn't want it to be never. But I knew that by next year I might not feel up to tackling a long journey. I'm more likely to spend my holidays in Torquay than in Australia.'

'That's nonsense,' Tony said. 'You don't look any older than when I saw you last.'

'I'd like to think that's true, though I doubt it. Old age has been creeping up on me. One creaks at the joints. Yet, oddly enough, I rather like it. Now tell me about Jan. I'm looking forward very much to meeting her. What's this job she's got?'

'She works in a kind of craft shop in the city,' Tony answered. 'A place where they sell pottery and handmade jewellery and so on. You'll see her this evening unless you'd like to go to bed and stay there. But my advice to you is, have a good rest this morning—I'll have to leave you to yourself and go off to work too presently—then if I were you I'd get up and have tea with us in the evening. Otherwise you may not sleep well tonight and it may take you days to adjust to the difference in time.'

Andrew knew that the meal which Australians call tea was what he would call dinner and at the moment he could not imagine himself wanting any kind of solid food for a long time to come. The meals that he had endured on the aeroplane had totally taken away his appetite.

'I believe you're close to the sea,' he said. 'I'm looking forward to swimming.'

'We're not five minutes' walk to the beach,' Tony replied. 'We were lucky to get the house. You'll see, it's nice. It was just what we wanted. And we didn't have to have a mortgage, we were able to buy it outright, because—' He hesitated and Andrew, glancing at him sideways, saw that he was frowning as if he were wishing that he had not said what he had. But with a sound of reluctance in his voice, he went on, 'Jan's got money. She inherited it from her first husband.'

'I didn't know she'd been married before,' Andrew said.

'Yes.' The way that Tony snapped his jaws shut after he had said it showed that he did not intend to continue on the subject. After a moment, however, he went on, 'You're going to stay with us for a fortnight, aren't you?'

'If you can put up with me for as long as that,' Andrew said. It seemed to him a very long time to exploit the hospitality of even the best of friends.

'Why don't you stay longer?' Tony asked. 'We could take some trips. The country round Adelaide is really worth seeing. And we can show you kangaroos and emus and other things you'd like to see.'

'Well, I've arranged to go to the Wilkies in Sydney,' Andrew said. Stewart Wilkie had been a post-doctoral fellow for a year in Andrew's department and had been as pressing as Tony that Andrew should stay with him and his wife on this visit. 'They're expecting me.'

'Still, we'll make some plans as soon as you've slept off the journey,' Tony said.

They were driving along a wide highway flanked by small bungalows standing in gardens in which oleanders, agapanthus and a spectacular red-flowering eucalypt were in bloom. The sky was an intense blue, a colour never to be seen in England and seldom even in the south of Europe. All the colours that Andrew saw seemed to have a brilliance in which he found it difficult to believe. With an English December only twenty-four hours behind him, he felt that there was a kind of exaggeration about them all that could not be natural. If he closed his eyes, he thought, then opened them suddenly, he would find that the tones had faded.

But he made an effort not to close his eyes, for if he did so, he thought, he would only too probably drift off to sleep, and it seemed only proper for the present to go on talking to Tony. He asked him how he liked his job and how he felt about the move from Canberra to Adelaide, and Tony said that the job was pretty good and that he preferred Adelaide to Canberra. No one who had ever lived in Adelaide, he stated, ever wanted to live anywhere else.

'It's a kind of sub-culture,' he said. 'It becomes a part of you.'

Then he asked Andrew how the book that he was writing was coming along and Andrew said, as he always did when he was asked this question, that it was coming along pretty well. But the truth was that he had been working at it for a long time and it had the strange characteristic that it never grew any longer. It was a life of Robert Hooke, the noted seventeenth-century natural philosopher and architect, and though Andrew worked at it regularly, paying frequent visits to the library of the Royal Society to do the necessary research, he found that as he went along he could not help destroying almost as much of it as he wrote. To himself he sometimes admitted that he did not expect ever to finish the book, and that he would not know what to do with himself if he ever did so, but to other people he stuck to his statement that it was coming along pretty well.

Having told Tony this, he went on, 'I've heard Adelaide's called the City of Churches.'

'That's right,' Tony said.

'And I've also been told that in spite of its being a sedate sort of place, more bizarre murders have happened in it than anywhere else in Australia. In fact, it sounded to me as if it could compete quite successfully with what we can do in Britain.'

Tony said nothing for a moment, then with an odd abruptness said, 'Who told you that?'

'I can't remember,' Andrew said. 'Perhaps it was Wilkie.'

'How long ago?'

That seemed to Andrew a curious question.

'Some years at least,' he said. 'It must have been before I retired.'

'It's true, of course.'

As if a kind of excitement overcame Tony as he said this, his driving accelerated. He was already driving at a speed that made Andrew nervous, though he tried not to show his uneasiness because apparently it was no more than usual on this busy highway. Other cars frequently passed them and on the left side as well as the right, which was evidently a local custom and perfectly legal.

'But what made you bring that up?' Tony asked after a moment.

'What? About the murders?' Andrew said. 'I don't know. No special reason.'

'That's true?'

'Absolutely.' Tony's tone puzzled Andrew. It had become uncharacteristically aggressive. 'It was a silly thing to say, but I never thought it would upset you.'

'It hasn't upset me.'

'I've a feeling it has.'

'Look, I tell you it hasn't. That's to say . . .'

'Yes?'

'Never mind. What would you like when we get in? Coffee? Bacon and eggs? A bit of steak?' With resolution Tony once more changed the subject and his face, which had had a strange shadow on it for a moment, which had looked almost hostile, regained its normal amiability.

Andrew said that what he would really like, if it would not be inconvenient, was whisky and a small piece of cheese. For a long time now he had had a habit of eating cheese with his breakfast. He could not remember when he had heard it or read about it, but at some time he had become convinced that it was healthful to start the day with some protein, and it was so much easier to slice off a piece of cheese even than to boil an egg. And at the moment it seemed to him that some whisky and some cheese would provide a satisfying compromise for his nervous system between breakfast and dinner, whichever his next meal should turn out to be.

They had been driving for some minutes along a road parallel to the seashore. The beach was a long, straight stretch of sand on which a few boys were playing cricket, but where there were very few other people about. Perhaps it was still too early for them to have come out. Only two or three were in the water. This was Betty Hill, Tony said, and Andrew thought that it must have been named by some early settler who had come from the north of Scotland, bringing the name of his old home with him, because there was nothing in sight that could possibly be called a hill. There had been dunes along the coast here, Tony added, but these had been cleared away and now there were bungalows along the edge of the beach.

The Gardiners' home did not overlook the sea, but was within a short walk of it. The road into which Tony turned was shaded with gums, with here and there a jacaranda, gloriously in bloom. Most of the bungalows looked fairly recently built, but the one in front of which he stopped the car looked as if it might date back to Victorian times. It was small and built of stone, with a roof of corrugated iron and a narrow verandah round it, roofed in the same way. Collecting Andrew's luggage from the boot, Tony led the way through the open gate and into the house by a side door that led straight into a kitchen.

Going through it and then along a passage that ran through the middle of the house, Tony took Andrew into a pleasant bedroom. The bed looked wonderfully inviting to him. He longed to get out of his clothes and stretch out on it immediately. But he had asked for whisky and cheese and by the time he had had a brief wash, combed his ruffled grey hair and decided against shaving until later, Tony had come to tell him that a drink and bread and cheese were waiting for him in the living-room.

Andrew followed him along the passage into a big, dim, square room, shaded from the sun by Venetian blinds and with an air-conditioner whirring in it. It was furnished with dark, solid Victorian pieces, probably collected with great care, for they looked good of their kind, though the general effect of them was somewhat heavy and sombre. But there were armchairs in gaily striped covers and green plants in pots on the window-sills. A tray with a bottle of whisky on it and some sandwiches made of bread and cheese had been placed on a low table beside one of the chairs.

Andrew dropped into it, remarking as he did so, 'That's a nice piece of quartz crystal you've got there.'

The crystal was on the table beside the tray. It was a strangely shaped object of a milky white, faintly translucent substance, looking rather like a collection of large jagged teeth joined into a bundle somewhat bigger than a human fist.

Tony smiled, picked it up and fondled it.

'Yes, it's nice, isn't it?' he said. 'I got it in an old quarry up in the Adelaide hills.'

'You dug it out yourself, did you?' Andrew said.

'That's right. I'm a bit of a rock hand. That's our name for the people who collect these things.' Tony replaced it on the table and poured out whisky for Andrew. He had none himself. 'That's one of the best bits I've found. I've found malachite too and tourmaline and garnets. And of course there are opals, but you have to have special mining rights to collect them. Crystal's my favourite.'

Andrew had begun on the bread and cheese. 'How d'you dig for it?'

'Any way you like, with pickaxes, hammers, anything. You find it in cavities in the rock called geodes—but of course you know all that. They're nasty looking objects when you first get them out, but you clean them in boiling hydrochloric acid and they come out like this. I can do it in the lab.'

'Lucky you've got a lab to do it in.'

'That's right. The only thing is . . .' The glow of enthusiasm that had been kindled in Tony's face for a moment faded. 'The only thing is, I don't do it any more. And I'm not sure about having the thing on show here. I know that in her heart Jan would sooner I didn't, but she won't say so, because—well, it's complicated really.'

Andrew watched him warily, trying not to make it too obvious that he was doing it with more than usual interest. He knew that there was something the matter with him. Having known Tony for a number of years, he was of the opinion that behind the façade of easy-going candour there was a great deal of reserve. On the surface he seemed the easiest of people to get to know, yet Andrew believed that even after all this time he knew very little more about Tony than he had when he had first come to London as a student.

'The fact is, there's something I want to tell you about, but perhaps it had better wait till you've had a rest,' Tony said. 'It'd be a bit rough to unload it on you now.'

14

'Go ahead,' Andrew said. 'I'm going to have at least a couple of drinks before I lie down.'

'All right, then. You see, the fact is . . .' But there Tony paused. Then in a voice that had suddenly become defensive, as if he expected some kind of attack from Andrew because of what he had to say, he went on, 'The reason Jan didn't come to the airport with me to meet you had nothing to do with her having to go to work. She never goes to work as early as this. She simply wanted me to tell you all about her before you meet each other. And she wanted you to hear it from me and not someone else who might give you a wrong idea about it all.'

'Is it something I've got to know if it's as difficult as all that to talk about?' Andrew asked. 'I'm not normally inquisitive.'

'That's what I said to Jan. I said there was no need to talk about it at all. But she thinks someone else is bound to tell you about it and she'd like you to hear the true story first.' Reaching again in an absent-minded way for the lump of crystal, Tony stroked it gently with his fingertips. 'I told you she was married before,' he said.

'Yes.'

'But what I didn't mention was that her first husband was murdered and that for a time she was suspected of having done it.'

Andrew sipped some whisky and wondered what he ought to say. After a little thought he said, 'But it's all been cleared up, I suppose, only she worries that suspicion of some sort has stuck to her. Is that the trouble?'

'More or less. She would have been suspected, in fact I think she might have been charged, if it hadn't been—well, if it hadn't been for one thing.'

'Has anyone been charged?'

'No.'

'How long ago did it happen?'

15

'About a year ago.'

It occurred to Andrew that Jan had not wasted much time in getting married again.

'Then if you're sure you want to tell me about it, go on,' he said, 'but there's no need to, you know.'

'All right. Well, it was up in the quarry where I dug this thing out a couple of years ago. Wilding was a rock hound too—Luke Wilding, her first husband. He'd a sheep station near the quarry—what we call near in this country. It was only about ten kilometres away. And he was a rich man and he and Jan had been married only about six weeks when he was killed. And there are people who are sure she was with him when it happened and that she at least knows who did it. Even now the police keep coming after her every month or two with new lots of questions and it drives her distracted.'

'And where was she really?'

'In her home.'

'Wasn't there anyone to say so?'

'No. There was no one in the house. One of the men working on the station said he saw her set out for the quarry in the car with Wilding. At least, that's what the man supposed she was doing, but no one saw her come back, and when the police arrived at the house to tell her that her husband had been found murdered she was there and told them he'd dropped her off at the shops in Hartwell—that's the township near them—and that she'd walked back after she'd done her shopping. It was only a couple of kilometres and she liked to walk.'

'Wasn't there anyone in Hartwell to say she'd been there?'

'No. That's to say, yes. But they swore it was much later in the morning than she'd said. Only it was an old man who ran a hardware store who said it and he got muddled up when the police started questioning him, so it didn't amount to much. She'd done the rest of her shopping in a super-market and you know what it's like in those places, you go in and out without anyone taking the least notice of you. So she couldn't produce anyone to give her an alibi. But, as I said, there was something—something rather odd—that made the police inclined to believe her.'

'You believe her yourself, that goes without saying.'

'Of course, and when you meet her yourself, you'll understand . . . I mean, Andrew, she couldn't hurt anyone, she simply couldn't, and the way the suspicion's lingered on is perfectly horrible.'

Tony's face had flushed and there was such distress on it that Andrew wondered whether it might not be best to stop him ploughing on through the rest of the story. That, as it happened, would have suited Andrew, for he would have liked nothing better than to finish his bread and cheese and whisky and go to bed. But he thought that in telling his story Tony was making some urgent appeal to him and that the best way of supplying the understanding that he needed was to let him tell the rest of it.

Nodding, Andrew asked, 'What motive, if any, is she supposed to have had? Her husband's money?'

'Partly, but that wasn't quite the whole of it,' Tony answered. 'You see, Wilding was a brute. Quite literally. He actually beat her up a couple of times after they were married. He could be uncontrollably violent. Afterwards there were always pleas for forgiveness and promises that it would never happen again, but they didn't mean anything. She'd made up her mind to leave him when the murder happened. And she'd told her father about it and he'd spread it around the countryside without knowing it would do her damage later. He'd always hated Wilding and wanted to get Jan home to live with him again. He's a possessive old bastard. Luckily he rather likes me, I couldn't tell you why, so he didn't make the trouble I was half expecting when she told him she was going to marry me and come to live in Betty Hill.'

'Does he live a long way off?'

'No, he lives in Hartwell. It's only a couple of hours' drive away from here. He's got a small vineyard and a few olive trees and a bit of citrus, but he's neglected it all for some time and I don't think he's got much to live on except his pension. I doubt if that worries him, though. He's been turning more and more into one of those solitary characters who don't care much about anything so long as they've got enough to eat and drink. Particularly drink. But sometimes he'll turn up here unexpectedly and start talking—there's no stopping him when he does that—for a couple of hours, then he'll go away as suddenly as he came. Jan's very fond of him. Her mother died when she was a child and her father was everything to her.'

'Did she inherit all her husband's money?' Andrew asked.

'No,' Tony replied. 'She's got a stepson. It sounds pretty funny, putting it like that, because he's older than she is, but that's the fact. She was Wilding's second wife and he had this son, Bob, by his first marriage. Wilding left the sheep station to him and divided the rest of what he had between the two of them. Still, it's a tidy sum, and of course, if she'd left Wilding as she'd decided to do because she didn't hold with sticking to a man who actually knocked her about when he got in the mood for it, he'd have changed his will and cut her out. So killing him instead of leaving him would have had its points.'

'Did Bob know she was going to leave his father?'

'I don't know. Why? What difference would it have made?'

'Only that as long as he didn't know, he'd a motive for killing his father himself, but if he did know it would have been worth his while to put off the murder for a little while, because then, I suppose, he'd have inherited everything.'

Tony shook his head. 'He'd an alibi anyway. He was a civil engineer in those days and he lived in Adelaide, but he was visiting the Ramsdens—that's Jan's family—and he was out with Jan's sister Kay at the time of the murder. It was thought at one time that he and she were going to get married and that would have made Kay Jan's step-daughter-in-law, which would have been a bit complicated, their being sisters. But in the event she married Denis Lightfoot, who's Director of the Marine Biology Institute here and happens to be my boss, and Bob's more or less engaged to a woman called Sara Massingham who owns the craft shop I was telling you about where Jan works. A lovely girl and a great friend of Jan's. I think you'll be meeting them all on Christmas Day. We're going to have dinner with the Lightfoots.'

'You mentioned something that stopped Jan being suspected,' Andrew said. 'What was it?'

Tony was stroking the crystal again. 'It's something no one's ever explained. I told you Wilding was murdered in the quarry where he was hunting for crystal. It's an old quarry that hadn't been in use for years and there's a sort of billabong at the bottom of it. Pretty often it's quite dry, only just then there'd been heavy rain recently and it was a few feet deep. And Wilding's body was found in the pool. Yet there was clear evidence that he'd been murdered on a ledge quite high up on the rock face of the quarry. He was killed by a number of violent blows on the head with a piece of crystal that he'd just dug out that day. Quite a find. It was there on the ledge and was bloodstained and there were other bloodstains there. And you see, while it's just possible that Jan could have struck the blows that killed Wilding, though she's on the small side even for that, the thing that she couldn't possibly have done was drag his body from the ledge down to the pool. Wilding was a big, heavy chap. But even if he hadn't been, she couldn't have done it.'

'I don't know exactly what a billabong is,' Andrew said.

'It's a sort of backwater that forms a pool when a river's overflowed its banks or changed its course. There's a river near the quarry, the Orbell, a small tributary of the Murray, and some years ago it overflowed and flooded the quarry, then receded again, leaving this pool behind.'

'But why should anyone have moved the body into it?' Andrew asked.

'That's the question that's never been answered.'

'Can you see any point in it?'

'No one can. If the person who did it was sufficiently ignorant, he might have thought the death might be taken for drowning, but what advantage would there have been in that? It wasn't as if it could possibly have been an accident, or if there'd been any attempt to disfigure Wilding in the hope that he wouldn't be identified at once. Not that that would have had much sense in it. He was too well known in those parts and so was his habit of working in the quarry for him not to be identified as soon as he was found. On the whole it looks like a case of senseless panic on the part of the murderer.'

'Had Wilding been robbed?'

'No, his wallet with a fair amount of money in it was in his pocket.'

'And they still keep questioning Jan?'

Tony gave a deep sigh and leaning back in his chair, gazed up at the ceiling with a look of strain on his face that suddenly added years to his age.

'There's a Sergeant Ross who won't give up,' he said. 'He's made up his mind she's guilty and he believes that sooner or later he'll find the clue that will prove it. I tell you, sometimes I feel as if I could kill the man with my bare hands. But you can see now why she wanted me to tell you all this before she met you. She can't bear to talk about it herself and she thinks some friend of ours whom you may meet while you're staying here may drop hints about it which you'll find a bit disturbing.'

'That doesn't sound like the best sort of friend to have,' Andrew said.

'No, but you know how it is. In itself, it doesn't mean much. It just gives people something to talk about. But

Jan's very sensitive on the subject and someone's sure to say something about it to you.'

'I don't wonder she doesn't like it. And I don't wonder that she doesn't seem to like having this crystal here in the room. If I were in a position like hers, I know I'd lock it away.'

'But that's where the complication sets in, don't you see? She feels if she did that it would look almost like an admission of guilt. She wants it understood that a chunk of crystal hasn't any special meaning for her.' Tony suddenly stood up. 'Now we've been talking long enough. I'm sure you'd like to go and have a rest. Don't get up till you feel like it. I'm going to the lab. I'll be back by lunch-time and so will Jan, but we can eat when you want to.'

Andrew was glad to stand up too and go back to his bedroom.

He did not think of unpacking. Simply to take off the clothes that he had been wearing for about thirty-six hours felt a wonderful luxury. He was only half aware of what he was doing as he stripped them off, leaving them in a pile on the floor, and tumbled into bed. But the room was very hot, with sunshine pouring in past the slats of the Venetian blinds and stripes of the brilliant blue sky to be seen between them, and after only a moment or two he thrust back the bedclothes and lay naked where he had dropped. Almost at once he fell into a deep sleep.

He was usually a light sleeper, subject to dreams, but now he was engulfed in a dark nothingness and when he woke he had no sense of how many hours had passed. It dawned on him, even in his drowsy state, that although it was still daylight and the room was as hot as ever and his body felt damp with sweat, the sunshine had gone and the room was in shadow. So he had certainly been asleep for a fair time. But when he looked at his watch he remembered that he had not adjusted it when he arrived in Adelaide and he felt too muddle-headed to sort out what the local time probably was. Australian time was about ten hours or thereabouts ahead of Greenwich mean time, wasn't it? But what did that matter? The thing to do was to get up and go looking for a clock.

All the same, for a while he lay still, feeling a strong inclination to stay where he was. But it occurred to him that Tony and Jan might have prepared a meal for him, might be waiting for him, and there might besides be a virtue in following Tony's advice and forcing himself to accept the Adelaide clock immediately, instead of remaining for the next few days in a timeless limbo. Yet the effort of moving felt almost too much for him. A small bathroom opened out of the bedroom and he thought that he would have a shower, then unpack a few things and get dressed. But even when he had decided to do this, he did not move.

Recollection of the talk that he had had with Tony before going to sleep gradually came back to him. A curious talk. And now one of the odd things about it that came back to Andrew was merely an echo of the way that Tony had spoken. He knew that Australians had a way of letting their voices lift slightly at the end of a sentence and that that sometimes gave the sentence the sound almost of being a question. A feeling that all the time that the two of them had been talking Tony had been asking a question began to worry Andrew.

It worried him because he did not know what the question had been, though he supposed that it signified a need for some kind of reassurance. When Tony had been a student he had had a way from time to time of coming to Andrew for reassurance and encouragement. Sometimes it had been about his work, sometimes about problems that he had encountered in the English way of life, sometimes about his not infrequent love-affairs. It had been out of the trust that he had shown Andrew in those days, together with the fact that Andrew had never been forward in offering reassurance and encouragement when they did not really happen to be needed, that their friendship had developed in spite of their great difference in age. And now the sense of something familiar in that questioning voice, of some demand being made on him, lingered disturbingly in Andréw's mind.

At last he got up and crossed the room to the shower. It was as he stepped under the spray of water that he asked himself the question: How completely did Tony Gardiner believe in the innocence of his wife?

CHAPTER 2

When Andrew emerged from his bedroom he saw on a grandfather clock in the passage that the time was five minutes past five. That meant that he had slept for even longer than he had thought. But the shower had done him good. After it he had opened his suitcase and extracted some cool clothing, a pair of cotton trousers, a short-sleeved shirt and canvas shoes, and dressed in these, after a shave, he had ventured out into the passage to see if there was anyone else in the bungalow.

At first he thought that there was not. It was quite silent and all the doors that opened on to the passage were standing open. So Tony and Jan had not yet come home from their work, he thought. Then he heard a faint plop and realized that it was the sound of a gas stove being lit. Walking towards the door from which the sound had come, he saw that it opened into the kitchen and that the person who had just lighted the oven there was a young woman, undoubtedly Jan.

Her back was towards him and she had plainly not heard him come to the door. He stood there for a moment, then said a diffident, 'Good evening.'

She started and turned.

She was about twenty-five, he thought, small, slender and fine-boned, with a pointed little face with delicate features which would have been very pretty if her grey eyes had not been almost too large. They seemed to take up more than their fair share of her face and gave her a staring yet remote expression, as if they were not really focused on Andrew. Her hair was straight and very fair and was brushed back from her face and tied in a pony-tail with a scarlet ribbon. She was wearing a short, straight dress of red and white flowered cotton, and scarlet sandals. Somehow she was not the kind of woman whom Andrew had expected Tony to marry. He had expected someone more robust, less fragile.

'I'm sorry if I startled you,' he said. 'You're Jan, of course.'

She came forward and held out her hand. It felt like a strange little bundle of bones in Andrew's grasp.

'Have you had a good sleep?' she asked. Her voice was soft, but high-pitched, so that if he had not been able to see her he might have taken it for the voice of a child.

'Splendid,' he said. 'I'm beginning to feel almost human.'

'It's a terrible journey, of course.' She turned back to the stove, opened the oven door and thrust a casserole into it. 'Some day I'll try it myself. We've been talking recently of a trip to Britain, but it doesn't seem quite the right time for it. We've a lot of things to think about, apart from our just having got married.'

Among the other things that they had to think about, Andrew reflected, was murder, but seeing her he found it difficult to imagine her lifting up a great chunk of crystal and beating her husband's brains out with it.

'Tony hasn't come home yet?' he asked.

'No, but he's due any time now.' She closed the oven door. 'Would you like a drink, or shall we wait till he comes?'

'Shall we wait?'

'If that's what you'd like. But let's go through to the lounge. It's cooler.'

He stood aside to let her pass through the door, then lead the way to the room where he and Tony had had their talk

24

that morning. It was a good deal cooler than Andrew's bedroom had been, for the air-conditioner was still whirring there and the roof of the verandah outside the windows shaded it. Wistaria climbed up the supports of the verandah in a dense green curtain.

Jan threw herself down in a chair and gestured to Andrew to take another.

'You've known Tony a long time,' she said.

'I think it's about twelve years,' Andrew answered.

'I've known him all my life. D'you smoke?'

'No, thank you.'

'Mind if I do?'

'Of course not.'

She reached for a box of cigarettes on a table near her. There was a jerky nervousness about her movements which made Andrew wonder if she had something on her mind or was simply very shy.

'Tony's trying to break me of the habit,' she said as she lit a cigarette and inhaled deeply. 'I don't know how often I've given it up, but I've no will-power. Tony has ever so much. You know that about him, do you? Once he's decided to do a thing, nothing can stop him.'

'Except that you still smoke, so something's stopped him there.'

'That's right, but that's different, isn't it? His strength against my weakness. When you get that sort of situation, weakness nearly always wins.'

'You've known him all your life, you said?'

'Yes, we both grew up in a place called Hartwell,' she answered. 'I can't remember a time when he wasn't there. He's ten years older than I am, you see, so by the time I began to take notice of things he was always in and out of my home because he hadn't any brothers or sisters of his own and it amused him to play with my sister and me. He did it so nicely that when I was three I made up my mind to marry him. I don't think I changed my mind about that till I was nearly grown up, when it slowly dawned on me that I wasn't quite as important in his life as he was in mine. He was always in love with two or three girls at a time, but never with me, so I gave him up and in the end got married to somebody else.' She gave a soft little laugh, but as she did so Andrew found that her great eyes were searching his with no trace of amusement in them.

He hesitated about what to say. His inclination was just to nod his head, perhaps to say, 'Ah yes,' and let her go on if she wanted to, to tell him about her marriage and its frightening ending, or else just to change the subject. But then he said, 'Tony's told me your story. I believe you wanted him to.'

She tipped some cigarette ash into an ashtray and seemed to relax, as if he had said what she wanted.

'Yes, but let's not talk about it now,' she said. 'Tony'll have told you all there is to know. I wanted him to do that so that if other people made what struck you as strange remarks, you wouldn't be puzzled. It isn't that we talk about it much ourselves. We've put it behind us—or tried to. Now tell me about your book. You're writing one, aren't you?'

'Let's not talk about that either,' Andrew said. 'It wouldn't interest you. Anyway, there isn't much yet to talk about and perhaps there never will be. Tell me about your job. Tony said you work in a craft shop.'

'That's right. It's in the city. We sell pottery and jewellery and a few paintings. You know the sort of thing. Most of the stuff is by local people and some of it is really nice. You must come in and look round one day. One or two of the people we deal with are really talented.'

Andrew said that he would love to go in and look round, thinking it sounded as if he might be able to buy two or three things to take home as presents for the few people who would expect it of him. He and Jan were still talking about the shop and she was describing with a gentle sort of mockery some of the really very odd people whose work they tried to sell in it—charming people, she said, because odd people, after all, were so much more attractive than the abysmally normal, weren't they?—when a car was driven past the window to a garage beside the house and Tony joined them.

They had drinks then and presently Jan left them to prepare the meal they called tea. They ate it at one end of the kitchen. It was a long, narrow room which at one time, Andrew thought, had probably been two rooms, but the partition between them had been taken away, giving a pleasant feeling of space in it. Tea consisted of a dish of crayfish, a casserole of lamb, and mangoes. There was a white wine with the first course and a red wine with the lamb, both of which had flavours that were strange to Andrew, but which he soon decided were very agreeable. His appetite had returned since his sleep and he was surprised at how well recovered from the journey he felt.

Tomorrow, he thought, he would swim while Tony and Jan were out at work. That was something to look forward to. He had been athletic when he was young, but now swimming and walking were the only forms of physical activity that he could enjoy and there was something particularly alluring about the thought of swimming in a warm blue sea in late December.

He was telling Jan that the mango was the most delicious thing that he had eaten for years when the door from the kitchen into the garden was suddenly opened and a very tall young man came in. He came in as if it were something that he was accustomed to doing without ringing or announcing himself beforehand and Jan and Tony showed no surprise at seeing him. Yet to Andrew he was a surprising sight. It was not only that he was very tall and very thin, with a mop of yellow curls, a pale face with a long, pointed chin, a long, sharp nose and singularly bright blue eyes that had a nervous, almost frightened gleam in them, but he was dressed in rags. It was the only word for them. He wore blue jeans that were more than usually dirty, a shirt that might once have been white, with a badly frayed collar open to his chest, and a grey pullover that had great holes through which his elbows protruded and the knitting of which had the general appearance of coming slowly undone. He was barefoot and had red varnish on his toenails. He looked about twenty-two.

Muttering, 'Hallo,' he started across the kitchen towards the door that led into the passage.

'On the chair by the clock, Dud,' Jan called after him.

'Okay,' he mumbled and disappeared through the door.

After a moment he reappeared carrying a bright green bundle under one arm.

'Thanks, Jan,' he said, and was about to return to the door through which he had entered the kitchen when she checked him.

'Come and meet Professor Basnett, Dud,' she said. 'He's a very old friend of Tony's who's arrived from England today.'

The young man seemed to pause unwillingly, indeed for a moment it looked as if he were considering bolting for the door, but then he turned, came to the table and held out a hand to Andrew.

'Good evening,' he said in a tone of great politeness. 'I hope you had a pleasant journey.'

His voice was unmistakably English. Upper class English. Perhaps even Eton.

'This is Dudley Blair,' Jan said. 'He's been making jewellery. We sell it at the shop. Very successfully too. It's really beautiful. You must come and see it.'

The young man gave an uneasy smile. 'I shouldn't bother. It's nothing special. Goodbye, Professor. I hope you enjoy your stay. Good night, Jan, and thanks again. Good night, Tony.'

This time he made it successfully to the door, went out and closed it behind him.

'What was that you gave him?' Tony asked.

'Only a beach towel,' Jan answered. 'I saw him on the beach the other day and the thing he called a towel was just a disgusting old rag. So I said if he'd call in this evening I'd lend him another.'

'Lend it, did you say?' Tony said. 'You'll never see it again.'

'Does that matter? We've got plenty.'

'You let him get away with too much.'

'Well, he needs someone to look after him. And he's talented, you know, he really is. I might not bother about him if I didn't think he was.'

'He's English, isn't he?' Andrew said. 'Where does he come from?'

'He's English and I believe he's an Honourable, or something like that, though he gets annoyed if that's ever mentioned,' Jan replied. 'But I'm not sure where he actually comes from. He turned up here two or three years ago and he lives on the dole and when the mood takes him he makes some really beautiful silverwork. He used simply to give it away because he couldn't be bothered with all the business of selling it, till Sara—Sara Massingham, she's my boss— took him in hand and persuaded him to bring his things to her. But I don't think he cares much about that. Suddenly he'll disappear and just go walking about the country like an Aboriginal, all over Australia, or he'll get a job of work, picking grapes, perhaps, and make enough extra money to keep him going for some time. He's a strange creature, but he's gentle and generous and I'm really very fond of him.'

'The silly young fool smokes pot when he can get it,' Tony said.

'So do a lot of the kids, the kind who bring their stuff in to us,' Jan answered back. 'Not much, because they can't afford it, but mostly they grow out of it before long. I suppose a few of them turn into real addicts and go on to heroin, but in general I think it's just a phase they go through.'

29

'Where do they get the stuff?' Andrew asked.

Tony shrugged his shoulders. 'I suppose the word goes around somehow. We've quite a drug problem in Australia. It mostly comes in from Indonesia and every so often you hear of the police making a big haul, but I suppose there are always consignments that get through.'

Andrew thought of the dog that had sniffed his luggage at the airport, a precaution he had never encountered at Heathrow, though Britain had its drug problem too.

'But that boy's work is really good, is it?' he said to Jan. He thought of all the students he had known whose work at first had seemed to show great promise, but who had then obviously lost interest in it, perhaps because they found that they had chosen the wrong career, or because they wanted a short cut to making money, or were simply lazy.

'It will be good if he really gets down to working at it,' Jan answered, 'but I'm not sure if he's got the stamina to do that. At present, I admit, he's still an amateur, doing things that sometimes really come off, but sometimes are just a mess.'

'Anyway, why can't he wash his own towels?' Tony asked.

Jan laughed. 'You know you don't mind what I give him. You rather like him yourself. You don't mind it when I try to feed him up occasionally.'

Jan and Tony exchanged a long look. There was amusement and a great deal of affection in her strange, over-large eyes and after a moment he responded with a smile. Yet there was something in their attitude to one another that worried Andrew. It seemed to him that there was something artificial about it, almost as if they wanted to make a display of their affection to make sure that he was aware of it.

'Like it or not, I know I've got to put up with him,' Tony said. 'Now let's have some coffee. I'll make it.'

He got up and went to the kitchen end of the room, filled and plugged in a kettle and poured coffee beans into a grinder. Jan stood up too and began clearing the table and stacking the dishes and glasses in the dish-washer. Andrew tried to help, but gathered that he was only in the way. All at once his fatigue had returned and he was longing to go back to bed. Jan and Tony saw it and as soon as the coffee had been made and he had had a cup of it they insisted that he should go. They were showing themselves to be considerate and perceptive hosts and as presently he sank once more into sleep, it struck him how fantastic it was that their lives should ever have been darkened by the long shadow of murder.

Next morning Jan brought Andrew his breakfast on a tray and told him that both she and Tony had to go to their work, but that they would be back, at least for a time, for lunch. In case Andrew wanted to go out during the morning for a swim she gave him a key to the house and directed him to the beach. Though he was still heavy with sleep, he thought that a swim was just what he needed. After a while, when he got up, he put on his swimming shorts and a shirt, took the key and a gaily coloured towel that Jan had put out for him, and set off for the beach.

It was a straight, narrow stretch of sand, with Norfolk Island pines planted along its edge, their dark cone-shapes making them look like a row of watchful, uniformed sentinels. Where there had once been dunes and now were bungalows a rocky wall had been built to keep the sand at bay. The sea was calm, with the small breakers along its edge sending only a light frill of foam up the beach.

There were not many people about. Some children were playing cricket and during the next few days Andrew discovered that at whatever time he arrived for a swim there were always children playing cricket. There was also a steady procession of joggers, who, like all joggers, had melancholy faces, their expressions inward-looking and detached from everyday life. There were also a number of people walking dogs, though a notice beside the steps that led down from the road to the sandy shore stated that dogs were not permitted on the beach.

A day after his arrival one of these dogs, who seemed to have lost his owner, took a deep interest in Andrew as he stretched himself out on the beach after a swim. The animal planted itself about six feet away from him and simply stared at him. Andrew attempted exchanging greetings with it. It did not respond but only went on staring. It made Andrew wonder if the animal did not understand English and was the pet of one of the Greek or Italian families who had recently settled in Australia. But the probability was, he thought, as at last the dog got up and walked away, that in spite of the showers that he had had and the number of times that he had been into the sea, strange foreign smells still lingered about his person in which the dog had been interested.

Yet already, Andrew realized, he did not feel foreign. Later in the day he took a walk along the main street of Betty Hill, where there were shops, a great many of them for takeaway foods, and restaurants and a hotel or two. There were also a remarkable number of obese people. They were of all ages, from the adolescent to the elderly, and surprised him because he had always had a picture in his mind of Australians as lean, stringy people, as their soldiers had been, muscular and tough. Perhaps, he thought, such people were to be found in other parts of the country among miners and graziers and sheep-shearers. But in the clement air of Betty Hill, ideal for tourists, which was plainly what most of these people were, they certainly did seem to run to fat.

Going into a stationer's, he bought a newspaper and the man who sold it to him instructed him kindly to have a nice weekend. Andrew thanked him and made his way back to the Gardiners' bungalow. He had a very nice weekend. Since Tony and Jan did not have to go to their work on the

Saturday or Sunday, they joined him in his morning swim, then on the Saturday afternoon took him strolling through the Botanic Garden in the city where he made his first acquaintance with the enormous Morton Bay figs. Two rows of them made a shady avenue and were so grotesquely shaped that they reminded him of Arthur Rackham trees that he had seen in picture-books in his childhood, from the roots of which gnomes, or it might be good fairies with wands and wings, would suddenly pop out to impart secrets much to the advantage of some wandering prince.

There was a lily-pond with great pink lilies just coming into flower and there were trees which at a slight distance looked like commonplace conifers, but which, on being approached, revealed themselves as being quite unlike anything ever seen in Europe. For almost the first time Andrew began to feel how very far away Europe was. The twenty-four hours that he had spent in the plane began to take on a new meaning. A world that was really intensely strange to him, even if its inhabitants behaved and spoke in ways that were more or less familiar, was spread out around him and delighted him.

Next day, after swimming and eating lunch in the garden, Tony and Jan took him a drive into the hills that surrounded Adelaide. They took him to the top of Mount Lofty, which had been the highest point that had been seen from the sea by some early explorers, and because of this had been given its name. On the way they passed a number of burnt-out shells of houses which had succumbed to a raging fire the year before. Whole hillsides had been turned black in that disaster when fires had swept down to the very edges of the city. But it was amazing and encouraging to see that trees were already beginning to regenerate and had tufts of green appearing on their blackened trunks.

At the top of Mount Lofty the three of them got out of the car and stood looking across the great sweep of fertile countryside, with Adelaide in the distance and a narrow blue ribbon of sea beyond it. Andrew thought how good it was to experience the sense of sheer spaciousness that this country gave you. When he was at home and had had more than he wanted of the company of his fellow creatures, there was nothing that he could do but retire into the small private world of his flat and make sure that he had closed the door behind him. But here it would be easy to discover all kinds of splendid solitudes. The thought thrilled him, even though he knew that the truth about himself was that he was able to endure isolation happily for only a few days at a time. He was really an urban man and would not for anything have lived anywhere but in London.

He had enjoyed these trips, yet there was something about them that had produced a curious discomfort in him. It was the sense he had of a strange tension between Jan and Tony. They were restrained with one another in a manner that was not in the least typical of Tony, who was normally a forthcoming, self-confident man. He seemed to Andrew now to be acting the part of a happy man rather than being one simply and naturally. Jan seemed more genuinely contented, yet even she sometimes cast sidelong glances at her husband, as if she were anxious about the impression that she was making on him.

He gave no sign of having observed the glances and always treated her with a loving gentleness that should have reassured her, except for the fact that it did not seem wholly spontaneous. Andrew tried to convince himself that he was mistaken in what he thought he perceived, but the suspicion that he was not would not leave him. He enjoyed Tony's company most when he had him to himself. Then Tony talked about his work, as he had in the old days, grew enthusiastic and seemed to forget that he had problems unrelated to it on his mind.

The day after the trip to Mount Lofty Jan and Tony went back to work and Andrew went down to the beach alone. The tide was low, which meant that when he went into the sea to swim he had first to walk a long way before the water was even up to his thighs. But at that point he plunged in and swam straight out to sea, still finding the slope of the sand under him so gradual that he had swum as far as he wanted before he was out of his depth. Presently he returned to the beach, spread out the gaily coloured towel that Jan had given him for the purpose and lay down on it to enjoy the sunshine.

The sun had already caught him a little. His skin was tingling and he supposed that he ought to be careful not to overdo it or he would find himself roasted and peeling. But it felt too pleasant there, stimulated by the swim and relaxing after it, to think of putting on his shirt as a protective measure. Slipping into a dreamy sense of well-being, he might have dozed if he had not suddenly been roused by the sound of an aeroplane somewhere surprisingly close overhead.

Opening his eyes, he looked up. A very small aeroplane was flying low down, parallel to the beach. It had a long streamer behind it which had on it an advertisement for somebody's rum as well as the statement that it was a shark patrol. Sharks. No one had said anything about them to Andrew since he had arrived at Betty Hill, which meant, he supposed, that they could not be any very serious menace. He would try to remember to ask Jan and Tony about it and was about to turn over and give his back a dose of sunshine when a jogger passed close to him and he was almost sure that it was Dudley Blair.

The reason that Andrew was not quite sure about this was that when he had seen the young man before he had taken more notice of his clothes than of his features. He would have recognized the disintegrating pullover anywhere. But this figure, tall and emaciated enough to be Dudley Blair, with ribs showing almost bare of flesh in his chest, was wearing only the briefest of shorts. True, they were dirty enough to be what he was likely to wear and he was barefoot, but he had passed Andrew too quickly for him to see if this man had varnish on his toenails.

He looked as sad as most joggers do, with his thoughts withdrawn into some private world which for certain was not very inspiring, or it would not have made him look so gravely remote from the scene around him. He either did not see Andrew or did not recognize him.

Soon after he had gone by Andrew had a second swim and when he returned to where he had left his towel and shoes, saw to his surprise that Jan was sitting there. She had left for work at the usual time that morning and was not due home for lunch for another hour.

'Hallo,' he said. 'How did you know where to find me?'

'I recognized the towel.' She had just lit a cigarette. Moving a little, she made room for him to sit down on the towel too. 'Have you had a nice morning?'

'Fine,' he said as he sat down. 'Tell me, are there sharks in these waters.?'

'Not that I've ever heard of.'

'Then why do they have a shark patrol?'

'I don't know. They've had one ever since I've lived here, but I've never heard of one being sighted.'

'What would they do if they did spot one?'

'I believe they sound a siren.'

'What kind of siren?' He thought of sirens in the war, the alarmist sound of the one that warned of the enemy approaching and the peace-bringing sound of the all-clear. 'Would one be able to tell the difference between it and an ambulance, say, or police or a fire-engine?'

'I really don't know. I've never heard one.' She smiled at him. 'But I don't think you need worry.'

'I'm not worrying, I'm just curious,' Andrew said. 'You're home early, aren't you?'

'Yes, I—I've had an upsetting morning and I thought I'd come home.'

'I'm sorry. Was it anything serious?'

'I suppose so, yes. Yes, of course it was.' She picked up

a pebble and began to draw lines on the sand with it, looking at the result as if she were really concentrating on it. 'That bloody man has been pestering me again. He goes on and on.' She tossed the pebble aside. 'Why can't he leave me alone?'

'Do you mean someone from the police?'

She gave a slight nod of her head.

'And they've been questioning you again about the death of your first husband?'

She closed her lips so firmly that it looked as if she did not intend to answer, but then she nodded again. Her fair pony-tail bobbed up and down. Andrew realized that she was very near tears.

'But do you mean the man came to the shop and cornered you there among your friends?' he asked.

'Yes, that's what he did. Sergeant Ross. But I told him I wouldn't say a thing to him there. If he wanted to talk to me he'd got to come to the house where we could be by ourselves. So he said, "All right," and that's where we've been for the last hour, till I couldn't stand it any more and told him to go. He really hadn't anything new to say to me, it's just that he thinks that if he goes on and on doing this sort of thing, I'll break down and tell him something that matters. I won't, because there's nothing to tell, but sometimes I feel like making something up, just to stop him doing this kind of thing. Perhaps he's counting on that happening, because then he could say he'd solved the case and forget all about it. It wouldn't matter to him that it wasn't true.'

Andrew supposed that that kind of thing could happen, though he was inclined to believe that it did so less often than it had recently become fashionable to think.

'Has this man any special reason for coming to see you today?' he asked.

She looked thoughtful, as if she were not really sure that she wanted to take him into her confidence. She drew almost fiercely on her cigarette. Then she said, 'Tony told you the whole story when you got here, didn't he?'

'Yes. Of course, I don't know how much he may have left out.'

'No.' She had picked up another pebble and was drawing a strange, abstract pattern with it on the sand. 'Did he tell you about my alibi?'

'I rather gathered you hadn't got one.'

'That's right. But I would have had if that old devil, Preston, had told the truth. He runs a hardware store in Hartwell. And that morning—the morning Luke was killed —I went into the shop and I bought some plastic bags for the freezer. I did that about nine o'clock, then I walked home. Luke had dropped me off at the store, then driven on to the quarry. And if Preston had told the truth about when I went into his place, they'd know I couldn't possibly have done the murder, because even if I'd really driven to the quarry with Luke, how could I have got back to the shop almost as soon as it opened? But Preston's stuck to it all along that I didn't go into the shop till about twelve o'clock, which simply isn't true. But if it were, you see, it means that I could just conceivably have done the murder, walked back at high speed—it would be about a three hours' walk—and then done my shopping.'

'Has this man Preston a motive for telling a lie about you?' Andrew asked.

'Nothing special that I know of. We've fallen out once or twice because he's got a habit of giving the wrong change, but I've always supposed that was muddle-mindedness and I haven't made much of a fuss about it. And perhaps that's what this trouble is, just muddle on his part. He may have mixed me up with somebody else, and the more he's questioned about it, the more stubborn he gets that he's been telling the truth, as stupid people do, I believe.'

'Wasn't there some sort of record of the sale?'

'Not one that told one anything.'

'But Jan, I thought from what Tony told me that the

police know you couldn't have done the murder. There's the matter of your husband's body having been dragged a long way, which they recognize would be quite beyond you.'

'I know, I know. But I get so tired of it and sometimes, I can't help it, I get frightened.'

Tears began to trickle down her cheeks.

'There,' she said, 'I knew this would happen sooner or later. Please don't take any notice of it.'

But it would have been difficult not to, for in a moment she had broken into convulsive sobbing.

Andrew rolled over on to an elbow, taking a long look out to sea, giving her time either to have a good cry or to recover herself, whichever it was that she wanted to do. Once the crying had been reduced to a few sniffs, he said, 'Jan, do you know who did it?'

'No.'

'Quite sure?'

'Yes.'

'Have you any suspicions?'

'That's something I prefer not to talk about. There's been too much talk of that kind already.'

'Yes, I see. But it sounds as if whoever did it did you a good turn. You've benefited in more ways than one, haven't you? Of course that's why the police keep on at you. Tell me, what made you marry Luke?'

She used the pebble with which she had been drawing the pattern on the sand to obliterate it in a sudden, swift gesture. 'Ignorance. Stupidity. Bitterness. Believe it or not of someone of my generation, I was completely ignorant of sex and what it can do to you. And he was very good-looking and had very attractive manners and I was so stupid I thought that meant he was gentle and understanding when the truth was that he was a classical case of paranoia. He got insanely jealous from the moment we got married and insisted that I'd got to submit to him in everything, and if

I didn't, he knocked me about. He enjoyed that. There was a very sadistic streak in him. I'd bruises to prove it. And bitterness—well, I told you I'd been more or less in love with Tony most of my life, but he just didn't seem to be aware of my existence. He was so used to my being around that he didn't bother to notice me. And I took for granted that he never would and simply accepted it as a natural thing that if I ever wanted to get married I'd have to think of someone else. And it seemed a good thing that Luke was as unlike Tony as anyone I could find. Then the irony of things was that as soon as I married Luke, Tony woke up to the fact that he hadn't wanted to lose me and that really he'd been in love with me all along . . .' She paused and gave Andrew a puzzled stare. It struck him that one of the strange things about her great eyes was that they hardly ever blinked. 'Why am I talking to you like this?'

'Didn't you come down to the beach, looking for me, because you needed someone to talk to?' he said.

'Yes, but that was about something different. It was about Sergeant Ross coming to see me this morning. I was so upset and so—so angry, so furious—that I had to explode. D'you know what that wretched old man Preston's been saying?'

Andrew had no need to say no, but she seemed to require him to say it, so he did so.

'He says there was another customer in the shop when I came in,' she hurried on, 'which there wasn't, and he says he's just remembered who she was. She was a woman called Mayhew. Mrs Maud Mayhew. She used to live in Hartwell and was a customer of his. And he says that she'll be able to corroborate what he's said all along, that it was about twelve o'clock when I came in. The only thing is, she's moved away to Sydney, which of course is in New South Wales, and if they want to bring her back to South Australia as a witness, they'll have to get extradition for her and it'll take a bit of time, even supposing they can find her. So really that man Ross came to see me just to try to frighten me and see if I'd crack when he threw this at me. I nearly did. I don't mean I nearly admitted anything, but I nearly started crying, just as I did just now, and in front of someone like him it would have been too humiliating. It was so horrible . . .' She gave an impatient rub at her eyes with her wrist, as if they had filled with tears again.

'If you don't mind going on talking about these things a little longer,' Andrew said, 'can you tell me what the police made of your husband's body having been dragged down from where he was killed to the billabong, or whatever you call it? What was the point of doing that? It doesn't make sense to me.'

'The only thing they've come up with,' she answered, 'is that whoever dragged him down was intending to get him into a car, to take him away and bury him in the bush where he'd never be found unless dingoes dug him up. But then either this person was disturbed before he got to the car by someone else coming to the quarry so that he had to make a bolt for it, or else he found he simply couldn't handle the weight of the body and just dropped it and made off. I can't think of any other reason myself. But now I'd as soon we didn't go on talking about all this. Let's try something else. Christmas, for instance. You know we're going to my sister's for our Christmas dinner, don't you?'

Christmas. It was only two days away. But not Christmas as he was accustomed to thinking of it. Not a white Christmas with big fires burning and holly decorating the rooms and with a spirit of festivity especially welcome because it broke the long depression of winter. The sort of Christmas which Andrew, who had neither children nor grandchildren, had in fact very seldom experienced, yet which, since his own childhood, had seemed the only authentic pattern of it. Instead there would be burning sunshine, a sky of incredible blue, shining sea and sparkling sand. Looking around him, he found it very difficult to think that this could really be Christmastime.

'Tony told me about it,' he said.

'They live quite near, only a little way down there . . .' She pointed at the row of bungalows built above the beach. 'You'll like Kay. And Denis is nice too. That's her husband. He's Director of the Institute where Tony works and Tony ought to take you to meet him. He'd be glad to see you.' Her mood appeared all in a moment to have changed completely. She was talking now as if all that she was interested in was a minor social matter. 'Kay's clever. I don't mean she's an intellectual sort of person. She doesn't read much or care about music or painting, but she's good with people. She's good at understanding what's going on in their minds. She can tell you what they're really like when she's only met them once or twice.'

'Is she older than you?'

'Three years. But I suppose because our mother died when we were very young I've always depended on her more than you'd expect with such a small difference between us. I think she's a wonderful person.'

Andrew wondered why Kay, if she was so perceptive, had not understood Luke Wilding enough to have warned her younger sister against him.

Sitting up, he reached for his shoes.

'Jan, tell me something and please be honest about it,' he said. 'I know you and Tony have your troubles at the moment. I knew nothing about them when I wrote and asked if I should visit you, and naturally I wouldn't have done it if I'd had a hint of the facts. But wouldn't it be easier for you now if I moved on and got out of your way? It must be a bother to have a stranger around when you've so much to worry about.'

She stared at him in her unblinking fashion. 'Do you *want* to leave us?'

'Of course not, I just thought it might be easier for you . . .'

She interrupted him by taking his face in her hands and

planting a kiss on his mouth. Then she jumped up and before he had finished tying his shoelaces had scampered away towards her home.

CHAPTER 3

Andrew put the same question to Tony later in the day. Would it be easier for him and Jan if he were to move on? The Wilkies in Sydney would not expect him yet, but Christmas, Andrew said, did not mean much to him and he would be quite happy to spend it in a hotel. Tony seemed astonished at the question. Of course, he said, he and Jan wanted Andrew to stay, to stay even longer than he had planned, as he had already suggested.

'The fact is,' Tony said, 'you're a help to us. Perhaps I ought to have let you know all about it before you came, but when we're by ourselves we either talk incessantly about Wilding's murder, or we're so careful to keep off it that we're quite unlike our real selves. I'm a suspect, you see, because I've married a rich wife, and pretty soon after her husband died. We keep coming back to the question of whether or not the police believe in my alibi. Actually I was in my lab in Betty Hill that morning, but I happened not to see anybody, and I'd time to drive up to Hartwell and could have done it without being seen.'

'What sort of alibi has Jan's father?' Andrew asked. 'He lives pretty close to the spot, doesn't he?'

'He's no alibi at all. He was working in his vineyard and there was no one to corroborate that either, and we go round and round that too. But you've brought something in from outside, for which we're very grateful.'

That was the end of the matter. Andrew stayed on. When

Christmas Day came he and Jan and Tony set off to join the festivities at the house of Jan's sister, Kay, and her husband, Denis Lightfoot.

Though the distance from the Gardiners' bungalow to the Lightfoots' was not great, they went by car. The Gardiners' car was a Holden, about seven years old. It had interested Andrew during the last few days to observe that although Jan was supposed to have inherited a good deal of money from her first husband, she and Tony gave very few signs of having more to live on than his salary. Andrew had been told that her work in the craft shop was voluntary and he recognized that although she acted as if she were a normal employee, sticking conscientiously to regular hours, this was mainly because she wanted it to be taken seriously. He had also encountered an Italian woman in the house who came in for a day once a week to clean it and whose wages were not small. And as Tony told him, they had bought the house outright, without a mortgage. But the house itself was small, its furnishing was good but not at all luxurious, and the car was old and even in its early days had never been a grand one. They had a second car, a small Volvo, but that also was several years old. Andrew guessed that this relative economy was simply because they did not want it to appear that they had profited by Luke Wilding's death. It must be well known that they had, yet it seemed that they shrank from making any display of it and might continue to do so until his murderer was found.

The Lightfoots had a much larger bungalow than the Gardiners, a modern one which overlooked the beach. The long window of its spacious living-room looked straight out to sea, which today was not as calm as it had been ever since Andrew's arrival. Small crests of white topped the waves as they came slanting in towards the shore, and the breakers there, small though they were, were bigger than he had yet seen them. But the sky was clear, the sunshine warm, the breeze that came in from the sea only a light one and the temperature was only a little less sweltering than it had been for the last few days.

As soon as he met his host, Andrew began to have an uncomfortable feeling that he was overdressed. He was in a light grey suit which he thought of as his tropical one, suitable for a festive occasion such as this, but Denis Lightfoot was in shorts, a brightly patterned, short-sleeved shirt and sandals. He was about forty-five, a man of about the same height as Andrew, who was six foot, and had an oval face with neat, regular features, grey eyes, good teeth which he showed in a frequent yet rather expressionless smile, and light brown hair that was already receding from his forehead. It was he who opened the door when Jan, Tony and Andrew arrived. He gave Jan a kiss, said, 'Hallo,' to Tony, grasped Andrew by the hand, said how glad he was to see him and led the way to the living-room to meet his wife and the other guests who had arrived before them.

The room was a long one, with pale grey walls, a white carpet, white curtains and light-coloured modern furniture. There was a fireplace with logs in the grate, but they had an almost sculptured look, as if they had been carefully arranged and no one had dreamt that they might ever be lit. On a low coffee table in the centre of the room was a big, milky-white chunk of quartz crystal.

Kay Lightfoot came quickly forward to greet Andrew. At a glance he could have seen that she was Jan's sister, though she was a good deal the taller of the two and far more sturdily built. She was a shapely woman, however, firm-breasted and small waisted. Her hair was of the same fair colour as Jan's, but had been cut short by a skilful hairdresser. Only her eyes were completely different from her sister's. They had not the over-largeness of Jan's, or the haunted look that dominated all her other features, but in their way they were arresting too, for they were very dark, in striking contrast to the fairness of her hair. They were watchful eyes, intent and searching. Not much, Andrew thought, would escape them. She was wearing a sleeveless dress of black and white cotton, which, simple as it was, had the subtle air of being expensive. If the Gardiners had inherited a fortune, even one of only moderate size, it looked as if the Lightfoots, by whatever means, had come into possession of more.

'We're so glad to meet you at last, Professor,' Kay said. 'No, I can call you Andrew, can't I? We've heard so much about you from Tony. He was thrilled when he heard you were really coming out to Australia again, and I said at once he must bring you to us for Christmas.'

Her voice was very like Jan's, as high-pitched though perhaps not quite as soft, and it made Andrew reflect that voices run in families even more than build or facial characteristics. If Kay and Jan had been out of sight, talking, he would not have been sure which was which.

'We're drinking champagne,' Kay said. 'Would you like that, or would you sooner have whisky or vodka?'

Andrew accepted the champagne and had a long glass put into his hand. Then he was taken to be introduced to the other guests. There were four of them, a young couple called Nicholl, a woman of thirty who turned out to be the Sara Massingham who owned the craft shop where Jan worked and who was what Tony had called more or less engaged to Bob Wilding, Jan's stepson. The stepson who was older than she was. It surprised Andrew a little to find him here now and to learn that he was actually staying in the house. However, if he was on friendly terms with the Lightfoots, and so probably with Jan and Tony too, all it could mean was that he was not one of the people who suspected Jan of being in any way involved in his father's murder.

Nevertheless, as Andrew chatted to the young man, who was tall, dark-haired, blue-eyed and uncommonly good-looking in a bony-featured, hollow-cheeked way, he could not quite put it out of his mind that Bob Wilding had benefited by his father's death as much as Jan. So why should he not be prepared to be on the friendliest of terms with her, even if he did not altogether believe in her innocence?

They talked inevitably about Andrew's journey and about whether or not he liked Australia, and Denis Lightfoot apologized to him for the climate being so hot, to which he replied that apart from the pleasure of seeing old friends, it had been the thought of the heat and the sunshine in darkest December that had drawn him back to the country.

Sara Massingham was almost as tall as Bob Wilding. She had straight black hair brushed smoothly back from her forehead, dark eyes and a narrow face with an exquisite complexion. She was very slender and was wearing green slacks and a green blouse with a delicate silver necklace at her throat. A beautiful woman who moved with grace as well as having a look of intelligence, though also of a certain remoteness about her.

An enormous turkey was served in a dining-room that had a cleverly designed pseudo-Georgian air about it. Andrew found himself seated on Kay's right with Clare Nicholl beside him. She was about the same age as Jan, a small, rather plump girl with short curly red hair and eyes that were really green. It occurred to him, meeting them, how the eyes that are called green usually are actually grey with only a faint tinge of green in them, but hers, smiling at him out of a round, plump face which was brown from the sun, were so green that they gave her an elfish look, not quite human. She might have been one of the strange creatures whom he had imagined as popping out to watch him from among the twisted roots of the Morton Bay figs in the Botanic Garden.

But her appetite for turkey was entirely human. After a first substantial helping she had a second, chatting to Andrew and to Bob Wilding, who sat on the other side of her, mostly about her garden and the fruit in it, the raspberries, the apricots, the strawberries which had already had one season and were now achieving a second, the beans and the zucchinis. Her chief interests seemed to be connected with edible things, which perhaps accounted for her quite pretty plumpness.

Her husband, David Nicholl, sat opposite her, between Jan and Sara Massingham. Andrew had been told that the young man was a colleague of Tony's working at the Institute of Marine Biology. He looked perhaps a year or two older than his wife, though this might have been the result of the gravity of his expression. He was of medium height and sturdily built and was either shy or naturally given to silence, for he spoke very little to either of the women who sat beside him. But when from time to time he responded to one or the other of them, he had a smile of singular charm. Like his wife, he did his duty by the turkey, reminding Andrew that at the young man's age he too would have been able to eat gigantically of anything so good.

He found it tempting to do so now, but he knew that if he did his digestion would make him pay for it. And if he yielded to temptation too often he knew that he would soon find himself putting on those extra pounds which at the age of seventy-one it was wisest to keep at bay. There had been a time, soon after Nell's death from cancer, when he had more than half hoped that a heart attack would put an end to the almost unbearable problems of loneliness, but gradually he had found that life had still something to offer him, so that keeping his weight down had come to seem simple common sense.

Not that there was any point in thinking too much about that sort of thing today. After the turkey came a Christmas pudding, a-flame. But between the two courses came a ritual which Andrew had never encountered anywhere but in Australia. There was a long, long pause during which people smoked, drank, talked and then all of a sudden decided to go for a walk in the garden. They filed out and went wandering round between the glorious jacarandas, the oleanders, plumbagos and hibiscus. Andrew found David Nicholl walking beside him. He seemed, from one of his small, sudden smiles, to wish to show friendliness to the stranger, but to have no words in which to do it.

Andrew could not think of anything to say either, but noticing Clare Nicholl on the path ahead of him, he remarked, 'Those are very pretty ear-rings your wife is wearing.'

David Nicholl's response was another of his charming smiles.

'You really think so? They're malachite which I dug out of the rock myself some time ago. I got the silverwork done by a fellow called Dudley Blair. A very weird character who sometimes hangs around in Adelaide for a time, when he isn't off walking on his own in the desert or North Australia. English and one of your real eccentrics, who have a way of turning up in Australia from time to time, looking for I don't know what, and God knows what he lives on, but he does some quite fine work.'

'I've met him,' Andrew said. 'So you're a rock-hound, are you, like Tony?'

'I used to be, but then—' He hesitated. 'I dropped it.'

'You got tired of it?'

'You could say that. No, that wasn't it. Something happened.'

'Something put you off it?'

David Nicholl darted a sideways look at him. 'Of course you know the whole story of the murder of Jan's first husband, don't you?'

'I think I know most of it by now,' Andrew said.

'Well, you see, I was the bloke who found the body.'

'I see, and so you don't like going back to the quarry.'

'That's it. I get the feeling I might find another there. Stupid, but it was a bloody unpleasant experience. I can't forget the way he lay there, half in and half out of the water.

And the blood . . .' He swallowed painfully. 'I've never been much good at blood.'

'Did you know him?' Andrew asked.

'A little.'

'I mean, did you recognize him when you found him?'

'Oh yes, though he'd been battered about the head in a way that may have been meant to hide his identity. But I knew Tony—we're in the same sort of job, you know—before Jan and Wilding got married and I used to go up to Hartwell with him sometimes and met Wilding there. And then we'd occasionally meet at the quarry. I recognized him at once.'

'What did you make of his body having been dragged down to the pond? Does it make any sense to you?'

'I can't say it does.'

'Jan told me that one of the police theories about it is that the murderer was dragging the body to a car to take it out into the bush, or anyway to conceal it somewhere, then he was interrupted by someone else coming on the scene.'

'I know.'

'Were you that person, d'you think?'

'I could have been.' The young man's answers were becoming increasingly terse and a deep frown had taken the place of the occasional smile.

'I'm sorry,' Andrew said. 'It's not a subject for Christmas Day.'

'My fault,' David said. 'I started it. And the fact is, it's difficult to keep off it, once you get started. They'll never find who did it, of course, unless they've got some evidence they've kept quiet about. I don't think they have, but it's always possible. If they haven't, it's too long ago now for them to come up with anything. But I don't like the quarry any more.'

'Where did the lump of crystal in the Lightfoots' room come from?' Andrew asked. 'Do you know that?'

'I think Tony gave it to them,' David answered, and as

if he had said all that he wanted to for the moment, the young man suddenly left Andrew's side and went ahead to join his wife.

Andrew found himself strolling along beside Bob Wilding, who had been walking with Sara Massingham, who had just left him and gone walking ahead by herself, moving with a long, graceful stride that had soon out-distanced everyone else in the party.

There was a slight flush and a look of excitement on Bob Wilding's hollow-cheeked face.

'So that's settled,' he said. He gave Andrew a slap on the back as if he were congratulating him for something. But as it turned out, the congratulations were for himself. 'She's agreed definitely at last. I found the right lever to make her do it. She's a lovely creature, isn't she?'

'Miss Massingham?'

'That's right. Isn't she lovely?'

'Very.'

'And it was quite simple really. All I had to do was promise to sell the sheep station and come back to live in Adelaide, and as I've been thinking of doing that myself for some time . . .' He paused. 'But you don't know what I'm talking about. I'm sorry. It's just that I've been trying for months to get Sara to agree to marry me and if she'd said before that being a farmer's wife wasn't her idea of bliss, I'd have told her right away I was ready to sell up any time. My father was very keen that I should keep the farm going, so I thought I ought to give it a try, but I'm not cut out for it.'

'So now you've told her that and she's happy?'

'That's it. Wonderful. Difficult to take in at the moment. I can't quite believe in it. I've wanted it so badly for so long.' Bob Wilding gave an abrupt, almost crazy-sounding little laugh that matched the excitement in his face. 'I suppose I oughtn't to be talking about it like this. She'll probably be crook at me, but I don't feel I can keep it to myself. If I hadn't told you, I'd have told somebody else. I may do that anyway. Then tell them all to drink to it, that'd be a perfect end to this fine dinner. But Sara might not like it. She always keeps her feelings to herself. I've never been sure whether or not she'd ever care for me. So now it's gone to my head a little. I'm sorry about that. I oughtn't to have unloaded it straight on to you, a perfect stranger. I expect you think I'm a little mad."

'I feel very honoured,' Andrew answered sedately.

'Yes, of course that's what you've got to say,' Bob said. 'But the truth is, ever since I inherited the damn farm, I haven't known what to do with it. I was an engineer, doing pretty well in an Adelaide firm, before my father died and left the place to me. I thought of selling it right away, but that seemed kind of callous. He'd been quite wrapped up in it himself and he trusted me to keep it going, which is why he didn't leave even a share of it to that damn girl . . . I'm sorry, she's a friend of yours, isn't she?'

'Jan?' Andrew nodded.

'There, that's the sort of thing I always do,' Bob went on, 'saying the wrong thing to the wrong person. I've nothing against her, you know. I've never believed the sort of thing people have said about her. But it's a difficult thing having a stepmother younger than yourself. I was very attracted by her once and had to forget about it when she married my father. And next it was Kay—yes, by God, I was really in love with Kay for a time. I was really upset when she married Denis, though we've always stayed friends. That's how it is I'm here today. I'm staying with them for a day or two. I invited myself and it was nice of them to let me come, but in the end, you see, it was a lucky thing for me she married Denis, because it was after that that I met Sara and this thing with her is quite another matter. I'd cut my throat if it went wrong. Are you married, by the way?'

'I used to be,' Andrew said.

'Ah. Divorced?'

'No, my wife died.'

'Oh, I'm sorry. But there I go again, you see, saying the wrong thing, quite the wrong thing, to the wrong person.'

'It doesn't matter.'

'But I ought to be more careful what I say. I've a way of saying anything that comes into my head. Perhaps Sara will cure me. She may manage to teach me some tact. She's got lots of it. Talking about my father and Jan, by the way, you know all about that, I suppose.'

'About his death, you mean?'

Bob nodded. The colour in his cheeks had subsided, but his eyes still had a slightly wild gleam in them.

'I think I've been told most of what there is to know,' Andrew said.

'Terrible thing. It's cast a shadow on us all ever since. There's no one here today who hasn't been involved in it to some extent except yourself. Even the ones of us with alibis have been made to feel that the mere fact of having an alibi can be suspicious. Isn't there something odd about remembering just what you were doing at just a certain time on a certain day? It would sound much more normal not to be too sure about it. But people who aren't sure envy the ones who are.'

'I believe you've an alibi yourself,' Andrew said.

'Who, me?' Bob sounded careless about it, considering what he had just been saying. 'Yes, Kay and I were out together, having a picnic in the nature reserve near Hartwell. I remember it because she chose that day when I was making up my mind to ask her to marry me—we were on the shores of a lake there, you should get Tony and Jan to take you to it, it's a lovely place with pelicans, kangaroos and everything—well, there we were and she suddenly told me she was going to marry Denis. Said they'd had a love-affair going on for months. I remember I said, "Is that right?" and she said, "Yes, that's right," and that's all there was to it. Then we got home and heard the news about my father.' There was a break in his hurrying speech. 'A shock, of course, the way it happened, but I never managed to pretend much in the way of grief. The truth is, he was a brutal bastard. I'd a sort of affection for him, I suppose, a kind of admiration because he was so tough, but he knocked me about like hell when I was a kid. If Jan knows anything about his murder, I don't blame her . . . No, I didn't mean to say that. How can she know anything? It's just because of the way people talk . . .'

As if he felt that he had said more than he had intended, perhaps because of the champagne and the wine that he had drunk with the turkey, he went hurrying ahead to rejoin Sara Massingham.

When he did so, however, she fell back and fell into step beside Andrew. She gave him her attractive smile and said, 'I know what Bob's been talking to you about, but please don't take him too seriously.'

'You aren't actually engaged to him, then?' Andrew asked.

'Yes. No. I don't know.' She laughed, as if she enjoyed the situation.

'He appears to think that you are,' Andrew said. 'If you aren't, it might be a kindness to put him out of his agony.'

'Poor Bob, he always lives in a state of agony,' she said. 'He rather likes it. He's very excitable. If he weren't really unsure of me, I think he'd soon lose interest in me.'

'I'm sure he wouldn't.' It was not merely a meaningless compliment. He thought her one of the most beautiful and arresting women he had seen for a long time and that she could probably do just as she liked with Bob Wilding.

'Ah, you don't know him,' she said. 'He's very unstable. And so am I, I'm afraid. I've accepted him in a provisional sort of way, but I'm not even sure if I want to get married at all. I think I'm in love with him, he's good-looking and he's rich and for the moment he's quite adequately infatuated, which are all very nice things, but am I in love with him? . . . Ah, good, I think we're being summoned to go in and eat the pudding. You won't say anything about what Bob's said to you, will you?'

She walked ahead again and slipped her arm through Bob's.

Neither of them said anything about any engagement even when the magnificent pudding had been eaten and the last of the wine in the bottles still on the table had been drunk. Andrew knew by then that the party were planning to swim as soon as the meal was finished, and although with so much rich food inside him he would not have been averse to having a short sleep before plunging into the sea, he did not want to be difficult about it. He and Tony and Jan had brought their bathers, as the Gardiners called them, with them in the car and when the party began to break up and Kay started clearing the table, Tony went to bring them in.

'I'll join you later when I've tidied things up,' Kay said. 'I shouldn't like to come back to such a mess.'

'I'll stay and help,' Jan said. 'It won't take long between us.'

'No, you go and swim, I'll stay,' Clare Nicholl said.

An argument about it developed among the women in which Sara Massingham did not join. She seemed to detach herself serenely from any necessity to take part in domestic chores. In the end it was Jan who stayed behind to help Kay tidy the dining-room and stack the dish-washer, while everyone else found bedrooms in which to change into their swimming things.

Andrew regretted the fact that he had not taken more of a liking than he had to Kay. She had been a charming hostess, concerned for the pleasure of all her guests, and Jan had told him that she was a wonderful person. But that was part of the trouble, for whenever he was told that of anyone he was inclined to expect the worst. He was always happier with understatement than with exaggeration, and after all, there were very few people who really turned out to be wonderful. Nice, kind, good, generous, affectionate, yes. They might have all kinds of excellent qualities. But to call them wonderful, he always felt, was going a bit far.

Denis took a large, brightly coloured umbrella down to the beach and erected it so that anyone who wanted to lie in the shade rather than in the full sunshine could do so. Andrew sat beneath the umbrella for a little while, then decided to go in swimming. Although the sea looked rougher than it had during the last few days, there was really no force in the waves. Striking out through the small breakers to the deeper water beyond them, he saw Bob Wilding swimming powerfully ahead of him, but most of the other members of the party had stayed where it was shallow, and presently Andrew found himself alone where low rollers with white crests swept past him.

He felt an immense pleasure in it. Letting himself be rocked by the waves, he stayed there for a while, seeing that the party who had stayed near to the beach were playing some kind of game which involved a good deal of splashing and shrieking with laughter. After a short time he swam back to the shore, waded out through the breakers and threw himself down on the sand, a little removed from the shade of the umbrella. Stretched out with the warmth of the sun on his skin as well as the coolness of the light breeze that was blowing in from the sea, in a few minutes he was sound asleep.

He had not noticed what the time was before he fell asleep. The long Christmas dinner had gone on until fairly late in the afternoon, but when he woke he saw on the clock on the tower of the Town Hall of Betty Hill, which was just visible from the beach, that it was a quarter past six.

He sat up and looked around him. Sara Massingham was lying alone in the shade of the umbrella, no doubt being careful to protect the whiteness of her skin. Clare and David

Nicholl were standing at the edge of the water, looking as if they were making up their minds to go into it once more. Andrew could not see Denis Lightfoot or Bob Wilding or Tony, though he saw some heads bobbing about some distance out to sea which were too far off for him to be able to recognize them, but he thought it probable that that was who they were. There was no sign anywhere of Kay or Jan. It was taking them a long time, he thought, to clear up the remains of the dinner.

Lying gazing up at the sky, he saw the white ghost of a full moon adrift in the deep blue overhead. It looked almost transparent, a mere puff of cloud with its sad face expressing as always a yearning for something that it would never be given. Andrew lay still for a little while, then thought that he would swim once more before the party decided to return to the house.

He passed David and Clare, who had just gone hand in hand into the water. He saw that Clare was not a very confident swimmer and wanted David to stay near her. But reaching the deeper water Andrew suddenly found himself face to face with Tony, who was swimming back towards the beach with smooth, elegant strokes.

He checked himself when he met Andrew and said, 'Had a good day?'

'Wonderful,' Andrew said.

'Time to be going in soon,' Tony said. 'We ought to be getting home. Where's Jan, do you know?'

'I haven't seen her,' Andrew answered.

'Having a kip, perhaps. Have you seen Kay?'

'No, but I've been asleep. They may have come down to the beach and gone in again.'

'That's right, I expect it's what they did. Well, we'd better join the others and go in.'

Tony struck out again for the shore. Andrew lingered for some minutes where he was, seeing the blobs of two wet heads still farther out, and assuming that they belonged to

Denis and Bob, he thought that there could be no reason to hurry if his host was still in the water.

But presently Denis came swimming in, with Bob close behind him, and the three of them made for the shore. David and Clare had already gone in and were sitting with Sara under the umbrella, though this was hardly needed any more. The sun was low and a tinge of faint coral pink had appeared in the sky in a line just above the horizon. The beach was emptying. When the party had first come down to it, it had been crowded with holiday-makers, some with umbrellas or tents, and a good many with the forbidden dogs. Children had been playing the inevitable cricket and from time to time the lonely jogger had slogged his way by. Now there were very few people left and the tide was slowly creeping over the sand.

'Where are Kay and Jan?' Denis was asking Sara as Andrew joined them.

'I don't know, I haven't seen them,' she replied.

'Been asleep, have you?' Denis asked.

'Not so far as I know. Perhaps I dozed off, but I don't think so. I don't think they've been down.'

'But there's Jan's towel over there,' Tony said, pointing.

A bright green towel was lying on the sand about twenty yards or so away from where the party had gathered around the umbrella.

'How do you know it's hers?' Denis asked. 'It could be anyone's.'

'Then it's exactly the same as some we've got,' Tony said. 'I noticed she brought one like it with her today.'

'But why drop it over there?' David asked. 'She'd have come here and joined Sara, wouldn't she? And what about Kay? Hasn't she a towel for herself?'

Something about the vivid green of the towel was familiar to Andrew, though at first he could not think why it was. Then the memory came to him of Dudley Blair slouching through the Gardiners' kitchen with a bright green bundle under his arm. But probably all this meant, he thought, if the towel was not Jan's, was that towels of that pattern happened to be popular in the shops of Betty Hill.

Tony had strolled over to where the towel lay and picked it up.

'I'm sure it's ours,' he said, returning.

'Then I suppose Sara did doze off,' Denis said, 'and Kay and Jan saw she was asleep and didn't want to disturb her, so they went in from over there.'

'But why did Jan leave her towel behind?' Tony persisted. 'Kay must have taken hers in and Jan left hers here. Isn't that peculiar?'

'Carelessness,' Bob suggested. 'She just forgot it.'

'Seems to me a funny thing to be careless about.' Tony seemed more disturbed by the incident than Andrew thought was warranted. 'It isn't like her.'

'Then let's go inside and see what's happened.' Denis began to struggle with the umbrella, trying to close it. At first it twisted in his grasp, then suddenly yielded, nearly trapping his head between its spokes. 'Time for a drink,' he said, emerging. 'Coming, everybody?'

Andrew felt that he had drunk enough for one day, but he would have to do whatever the Gardiners wanted, so he joined the group that trailed slowly up to the bungalow. Tony took the green towel with him, then as if he had suddenly become uncertain that it was actually Jan's, took it back to the spot where he had found it and dropped it there. Rejoining the party, he walked up the steps to the road beside Andrew.

Reaching the bungalow with Denis leading the group, they found the front door standing open.

Denis paused in the doorway and called out, 'Kay!'

There was no answer. Inside the house there was only silence.

Stepping inside the door, Denis called out again, but again there was no answer.

Looking round at the knot of people behind him, he said, 'They were probably caught by our neighbours. Probably they had to go in and say Merry Christmas to the kids. They've got a gang of them there. Not bad kids, actually, and Kay's fond of them. She'd go in any time if they asked her. Get out of your bathers now, then come along to the lounge for that drink.'

He walked towards the bedroom.

Andrew went to the room where he had left his clothes and stripped off the swimming trunks that he was wearing. The room was a bedroom and the clothes in which he had arrived were in a heap on the bed. Bob Wilding had shared the room with him. His clothes were on the floor.

Following Andrew into the room, he stood still in the doorway, saying, 'D'you know, I've never cared for Christmas? There's always a sort of disappointment about it, once you've grown up.'

'That's true,' Andrew agreed. 'It doesn't seem to mean much unless you've got children. It's just a time for drinking and over-eating.'

Bob closed the door behind him and picked up a shirt from the floor.

'Not that I've anything against over-eating if it's good enough,' he said, 'and Kay's a splendid cook. I wonder if Sara can cook. It's something I've never thought about. I can't imagine her standing at a kitchen stove. Look here, I didn't mean to tell you as much about her and me as I did, it's just that I was too excited to keep it to myself. You don't mind saying nothing about it to the others, do you?'

Andrew wondered if Bob was having second thoughts about the marriage, or if he had become less sure than he had been at first that Sara's acceptance of him had been serious. On the other hand, Andrew remembered that when he had first become engaged to Nell, all of forty years ago, he had had a feeling that no one must be let into the secret of it, that it was something too precious to be shared with anyone, that they must wait in silent enjoyment of one another before the right time came for making the matter public to their friends.

He and Bob were half way into their clothing when they heard a wild shout from the passage.

If it had been a woman's voice it would have been a scream. But it was a man's voice and sounded more like the roar of an animal in pain.

Doors on to the passage were opening. The noise had come from the living-room. Bob Wilding reached it first, then recoiled violently in the doorway, treading on the feet of Tony, who was just behind him. Clare and David Nicholl were close behind Tony, with Andrew joining the group which was trying to surge into the living-room, only to become motionless at what they saw before them. Sara Massingham had not appeared, as if roars of anguish did not mean much to her.

It had been Denis who had shouted. He was on his knees, beside Kay's prostrate body. There was blood on his hands and some smeared on his face, though he did not appear to have been injured. It seemed that he must have taken his head in his hands, after staining them in the blood that had gushed from Kay's battered head. Her face had been smashed in, though one sightless eye had been left peering out through the ruins of it with a dreadful, bright knowingness. Her fair hair had been stained red and there were thickening splashes of red on her black and white dress.

Lying on the floor beside her, with blood giving it a sickening pinkish colour, was the lump of quartz crystal that Andrew had noticed earlier on the coffee table.

Denis gave another yell, looking at the group in the doorway as if he hated all of them. His cry sounded as if he were trying to enunciate words, but could only produce this strange animal bellow. Then all at once he sat back on his heels and with a calmness that sounded a little mad after the noise that he had just been making, observed, 'I went to our room and changed. I came in here and found her. I found her just like this. I haven't touched her. I swear to God I haven't touched her. I didn't do it.'

David Nicholl went forward and put a hand on Denis's shoulder, trying to raise him to his feet. Denis only shrugged him off. David's face, always grave, was harrowed now by anxious sympathy.

'No one thinks you did it, Denis,' he said. 'You couldn't have, that's for sure. Her blood's already beginning to clot. Someone else got in and—'

'Where's Jan?' Tony interrupted suddenly.

They all looked at one another, as if the answer was to be found in one of their faces.

Turning swiftly, Tony went rushing from room to room, calling out, 'Jan! Jan, where are you?'

There was no answer. After a minute Tony returned.

'She isn't here,' he said. 'Her clothes are there in the room where we changed, but she's gone.'

'What about her bathers?' Clare Nicholl asked. She and her husband seemed to be keeping their heads better than anyone else in the horror of the situation.

'I don't know, I didn't think about them,' Tony answered.

'Go and see if they're there,' Clare said.

Turning once more, Tony darted into the bedroom where he had just changed. When he returned he looked extremely pale and bewildered.

'Gone,' he said.

'What about her towel?' David asked.

'Gone too. And that sort of beach robe she had.'

'So that towel you found on the beach could have been hers,' Bob said.

'But where is she?' Tony demanded, as if he thought that someone there could tell him. 'If she went down to the beach, what's happened to her?'

'If she swam out to sea . . .' Bob began, then stopped abruptly. 'I'm sorry, Tony. I'm sure Jan's all right. She's a strong swimmer. Even if she did swim out, she'll be all right. But Kay—oh God, I don't know what to say about it or what we ought to do. Get the police, I suppose.'

'I'm going to see if our car's still here,' Tony cried. 'I don't believe Jan went in swimming. If she had, she'd be back by now.'

He made for the front door and for the drive where the cars were parked in which the Lightfoots' guests had arrived.

As he went Sara Massingham thrust her way through the group who were still clustered just inside the doorway. Her face was paler than usual, but she had not lost her look of quiet self-control.

'We'd better ring the Triple O,' she said. 'I'll do it.'

CHAPTER 4

She picked up the telephone and dialled.

Andrew saw that what she dialled were three noughts, consecutively.

David, who was standing near him, said, 'You'd dial 999, wouldn't you?'

'It's the same thing, is it?' Andrew said.

'Yes, I think so. I believe the call will go through to the communications centre and they'll send a patrol. After that —well, I've never been involved in anything like this. I don't know what happens.'

Sara had spoken incisively into the telephone, summoning whoever it was whose job it was to deal with murder, then put the instrument down.

Andrew, to his own irritation, found himself reciting in his head:

> '"Pibroch of Donuil Dhu,
> Pibroch of Donuil,

Wake thy wild voice anew,
Summon Clan Conuil . . ."'

How much easier for Donuil Dhu it would have been, he
reflected, if he could have relied on the telephone to summon
his clansmen, instead of on the skirl of the bagpipes. They
would have arrived in half the time that it must have taken
them to reach the place from which they were to set off to
capture someone else's cattle, or whatever it was that their
chief expected of them.

On this occasion Clan Conuil, that was to say two uniformed constables in a white car with a blue light on top,
arrived in what seemed to be only a few minutes after Sara
had telephoned the Triple O.

But before they came Clare and David had led Denis into
the dining-room, had made him sit down there, had found
brandy in a cupboard of the sideboard and had made
him drink it. He had started to tremble violently and
when he drank the brandy it looked at first as if it might
make him vomit, but then it seemed to help him to
achieve some control of himself. When the two constables
arrived he insisted on going to the door to meet them
and led them into the living-room, instead of leaving this
to Bob Wilding, who appeared prepared to do the job.
The men stood side by side, looking down at Kay's battered head, then looked at each other questioningly and
then both nodded. One of them spoke into a radio which
was hanging on his chest and the radio clucked back at
him.

'That's the supervising sergeant I was speaking to,' he
said to Denis. 'It won't take him long to get here. Meanwhile,
if you don't mind, you'd all better go to that other room.
We don't want anything touched here.'

The two men herded everyone into the dining-room, then
placed themselves as sentinels in the passage.

Tony spoke in a low voice to Andrew. 'Jan didn't take

our car. It's there still. If I'd stopped to think, I'd have known it would be, because I've got the key. It's in my pocket. So God knows what's happened to her.'

'Perhaps she saw what happened here, got frightened and made a bolt for it,' Andrew suggested.

'In that case, why didn't she just run down to the beach and tell us about it?' Tony asked.

'Yes, that's what you'd have expected.'

'But there's that towel on the beach, as if she did run down . . .' Tony gave a shuddering sigh, then shook his head. 'No, she can't have gone into the sea, because her beach wrap is missing. It's a sort of jacket, made of towelling, and she'd probably have put it on over her bathers to go down to the beach, but if she'd gone in swimming she'd have left it with her towel. Anyway, why should she have gone dashing into the sea after seeing Kay killed, or on coming on her body after it had been done? She'd never have done that, would she?'

'It doesn't seem likely,' Andrew agreed. 'But just suppose she went down to the beach before Kay was killed, she might have left the towel and the wrap there together, mightn't she, then come out, put on the wrap, forgotten about the towel, come up here—'

'Yes, and then?' Tony interrupted. 'Then she found Kay's body and went rushing frantically away instead of coming down to us. That would be madness.'

Andrew looked thoughtfully at Tony's white face. 'What do you think happened, Tony? You've some idea about it, haven't you?'

'I can't think where she could have gone, except home,' Tony answered. 'But why should she have done that? I suppose it's just possible that something frightened her so that she completely lost her head and didn't know what she was doing. If she felt it was that other murder repeating itself, because she's never really got over it, you know . . . Anyway, I'm going to tell these men about it and see if they'll let me go home to see if she's there.'

He went out of the room to speak to the two constables in the passage.

Andrew, who had never felt such a stranger in the country as he did just then, with no justification for his presence in this house except through his connection with Tony, followed him out and heard him trying to explain himself lucidly to the policemen.

'Don't you understand, my wife's disappeared?' he said. 'She's Mrs Lightfoot's sister and when the rest of us went down to the beach to swim in the afternoon she stayed behind to help her sister clear up. And now she's missing. But her clothes are here, she's in her bathers, and her towel's on the beach, but I don't believe she went into the sea. I think she may have lost her head and gone home and I'd like to go there myself and see if that's what's happened. I can take the car and get there and back in a few minutes.'

'She didn't take your car herself?' one of the men asked.

'No,' Tony said. 'I had the key.'

'How far away is your home?'

'On foot? Perhaps ten minutes.'

'Have you any reason for thinking she might have gone there?'

'Only that she may have lost her head completely at seeing what had happened and felt home was the best place to be.'

The two men looked at each other and seemed to consult silently, then the one who had spoken before said, 'Ten minutes is quite a while for your head to stay lost, even if you've had a bad shock. Don't you think she'd be back here by now even if she started off for home? Why not telephone first to see if she's got there?'

Tony plainly welcomed the suggestion, picked up the telephone and dialled while the two men stood close to him, ready to listen if there should be an answer. But there was none. When the ringing tone had gone on for a longer time than it is usual to wait for a response on a telephone, Tony put it down.

'She might not be answering,' he said. 'She may be there. If I go, I can be sure. She's got to be somewhere. She can't just have vanished into thin air.'

'I'll tell you what we'll do,' the constable said. 'We'll wait till the sergeant gets here and tell him what's happened, then he can send one of us with you to see if she's at home. I don't think any of you should leave here till he's agreed to it. What's the address?'

Tony told him and the man wrote it down in a notebook.

However, when the superintending sergeant arrived a few minutes later, he did not give Tony permission to go home in search of Jan, but sent one of the constables to look for her. The sergeant, who was in uniform, was a big, burly man with sandy hair and small, shrewd eyes in a very large face. He remained stooping over Kay without touching her for some time, then nodded as if in answer to some question that no one had asked him, straightened up and on his radio asked the communications centre to contact the Divisional Detective-Inspector on duty, the major crime squad and the CIB.

After that he went into the dining-room where David Nicholl had persuaded Denis to drink more brandy and had poured out some for everyone else. Andrew was not sure that it was the best treatment for Denis. A flush had replaced his pallor and his eyes had an unfocused look, while his body was shaken every little while by starts and tremors. But Andrew was glad enough of the brandy himself. It was only as it was given to him and he looked round to see if Tony also had a glass of it that he discovered that he was not in the room.

So perhaps he had made off for his home without permission. The thought that he might have done this worried Andrew. Tony's intense anxiety about Jan was understandable, but it was not going to help matters to antagonize the police at the very beginning of their inquiry. The sergeant looked a level-headed man and his greeting of Denis was sympathetic, but the way he glanced round the room looked as if he was aware already that someone was missing.

'Sergeant Ross will be here shortly,' he said to Denis. 'I believe you know him.'

Andrew remembered that Ross was the name of the detective of whom Jan had told him, who had tried only a few days before to persuade her to change the story of her alibi.

'Ross?' Denis said vaguely and shook his head. 'I don't think so . . . Oh, I know, he questioned my wife about something to do with Luke Wilding's murder. I never met him myself. She wasn't my wife then. We've only been married six months. But she told me all about it, of course, and I think she said the man's name was Ross. Isn't that right, Bob?'

He turned his glassy, wandering gaze on Bob Wilding.

Bob nodded without answering.

At that moment Tony walked swiftly into the room, holding a bright green towel out before him.

'Look,' he said, 'there's blood on it.'

The sergeant stared at him, said nothing for a moment, then asked, 'Where did this come from?'

'From the beach,' Tony said. 'I think it's my wife's towel. Anyway, it's one of ours. We've several like it and I know she brought one of them with her today.'

'And you found it on the beach?'

Tony nodded.

'You shouldn't have touched it,' the sergeant said.

'And had it nicked?'

'You could have told us about it and I could have sent one of the men down to get it.' The sergeant held out his hand for the towel. 'Whereabouts on the beach was it?'

'Twenty yards or so from where we were all sitting under an umbrella we'd taken down.'

'It was just lying there on the beach?'

'Yes.'

'Didn't you see who dropped it?'

'No.'

'Isn't that kind of queer?'

'I don't know. Maybe. We all went in to swim more than once, except, I believe, Miss Massingham, so someone could have gone into the water without being noticed and dropped the towel there where we found it.'

The sergeant was holding the towel out in front of him and was looking it over with care.

'That certainly looks like blood,' he said, indicating a red smear. 'But it'll have to be tested. Miss Massingham, if you stayed there on the beach, didn't you see who dropped it?'

She shook her head. 'You know what it's like there in the afternoon on any holiday. There were people coming and going all the time. I wasn't paying much attention to them. I wasn't asleep, but I was in a kind of dream. And I didn't pay any attention to the towel either. I hadn't seen it before. Ask Professor Basnett if he noticed anything. He lay there on the beach for quite a time.'

The sergeant turned to Andrew. 'Did you see anything, Professor?'

'I'm afraid I was sound asleep,' Andrew answered. 'For quite a time, I believe.'

'So you're saying someone could easily have come down from this house,' the sergeant said, 'wrapping himself in this towel, perhaps even draping it over his head so that he shouldn't be recognized, then dropped it and gone into the sea to wash the blood off that he got on to himself when he was committing the murder. But he didn't realize there was blood on the towel. Is that your story?' His voice had become increasingly sceptical.

'It isn't a story,' David Nicholl said. 'It's what must have happened.'

'And where's my wife?' Tony suddenly shouted. 'How much longer is it going to take you to find her?'

At that moment the telephone rang.

Denis started automatically towards it but the sergeant checked him.

'I'll take it,' he said.

He picked up the telephone, grunted into it, then said, 'I see. Yes. Yes, come back.' Apparently the call had been made to him. He listened for a moment while a voice went on speaking, then he repeated, 'Yes, come back.'

Putting the telephone down, he turned to Tony.

'It looks as if your wife went home,' he said, 'took your second car and drove off. You have a second car, haven't you? My man says there are tyre marks in the garage.'

'Yes,' Tony said. 'A Volvo.'

'What's its number?'

Tony told him and the sergeant wrote it down in his notebook.

'Can you tell me where she'd be likely to go in the circumstances?' he asked.

Tony shook his head. But there had been an instant's hesitation before he did so which Andrew knew him well enough to have noticed. However, Tony's voice was firm as he answered, 'I still don't understand why she didn't come down to us on the beach if she'd seen the murder, or even if she only found her sister's body after the murderer had gone. Wouldn't it have been the natural thing for her to do? So isn't it probable that someone forced her to leave? And now God knows what he's done to her. I think he's killed her.'

'If that happened,' the sergeant said, 'and I'm not saying it's impossible, it means someone came in who isn't one of you here. I understand none of you who had your Christmas dinner here today is missing, except Mrs Gardiner. But before we settle on the tramp who dropped into the house when he thought it was empty to see what he could scrounge, I'd like to ask if any of you has any idea who else might have hated these two sisters enough to kill them both. Any suggestions?'

Silence greeted him. Then the doorbell rang.

★

In the confusion that followed, which was not really confusion but a singularly orderly process of men going about the work that they had come there to do, and which only seemed to be confusion because there were so many of them, Andrew found himself puzzling how the body of Jan, if she had been murdered, like her sister, could have been removed from the house, taken to the Gardiners' garage and then driven away. It was fairly certain, he thought, that she had left the house on her own feet. Perhaps she had had a gun at her back and had been forced by the murderer to go to her own home, get into the Volvo and drive the two of them to some fairly distant spot where he could commit his second murder and hide her body. In other words, it seemed possible that he had done almost what the murderer of Luke Wilding had tried to do, except that on that occasion it had been a dead man whom the murderer had been hauling towards his car, and the place had been a very lonely one.

The men who had crowded into the house were photographers, fingerprint specialists, a government pathologist and a plainclothes detective who Andrew discovered was Sergeant Ross. He was attended by a plainclothes constable and appeared to have taken charge. The uniformed sergeant who had appeared first had departed after making a report to Sergeant Ross, who was a tall, gaunt man of about forty and at first sight gave a misleading impression of being too thin, too lightly built to be strong enough for his kind of employment, but who in fact moved with the resilience that comes only from powerful and well coordinated muscles. He had a high, narrow forehead, a pointed nose and a long, firm chin. His hair was a light brown that almost matched the brown of his skin. His mouth was slightly crooked, with one corner of it lifted in what looked like a permanent sardonic, sceptical half-smile, though the expression of his grey eyes was sombre.

For a time he moved about the house, surrounded by the

other men who had arrived before him, but at last, while they were still going about their work, mostly in the living-room and the kitchen, he settled down in a small room that Denis used as a study, and sent the constable who had arrived with him to ask first Denis, then Tony, then one by one all the others who had had their Christmas dinner there that day, to come to be questioned.

Andrew guessed that he would probably be the last of these. He was a stranger. Except for Tony, he had never met any of the party before that morning. He had nothing to tell the police and probably they realized this. Sitting in a corner of the dining-room, he did his best not to get in anybody's way. If Tony had wanted to talk to him he could have joined him there. But while Denis was being questioned Tony kept walking about the room, sometimes moving his lips as if he were muttering to himself, and giving no one a chance to talk to him.

David and Clare Nicholl, however, came to sit with Andrew in his corner. One sat on either side of him. There was something protective in their attitude as if they felt that at his age and being a foreigner he might not be able to look after himself in the horror that had come upon them.

With the strange green eyes in her plump little face looking almost apologetic, Clare gave him a smile and said, 'If they weren't so busy in the kitchen looking for fingerprints and things I'd go and make us some sandwiches. There's plenty left on that turkey. You must be very hungry by now.'

Though he felt that there was something fundamentally sound about someone who put food before all other considerations even at a time like this and who wanted to be sure that others had everything they needed, Andrew answered, 'Thank you, Clare, but I don't believe I could eat even a sandwich. But don't let me stop you if you want something yourself.'

At the Nicholls' age, he thought, it was probably far more difficult to go without sustenance for any length of time than it was at his.

But Clare gave her head a worried shake. 'Is it those men in there, spreading their powders everywhere, who put you off the thought of food? If I brought the turkey and some bread and butter in here, wouldn't you like a sandwich then?'

'No, thank you,' Andrew said. 'I find murder takes the edge off one's appetite.'

'I suppose it does,' she said uncertainly, as if that were an experience that she had never had. 'What about a drink, then?'

'That I could do with,' he replied.

David got up, went to the sideboard and brought more brandy and glasses out of a cupboard. Pouring out drinks for the three of them, he said as he sat down again beside Andrew, 'This is very hard on you. I mean, coming out here for what you thought would be just a good holiday and have things go crook on you like this. You'll be able to get them to let you go, I should think, once they've checked if you saw anything this afternoon. You didn't, I suppose.'

'Except when I was swimming, I spent most of the time asleep,' Andrew said. 'But don't you think they'll expect me to stay for the inquest?'

David gave a derisive laugh. 'The inquest? That may not happen for several months. And then there may be another one after that. Or there may not be one at all. Sometimes there isn't if it's a certain fact that there's been a murder, and there can't be much doubt about that today, can there? What the police like to do is to wait till they're sure what the verdict's going to be and only bring a charge after that when there's no risk that it might be innocent, because if it were of course there couldn't be another trial.'

'Was there an inquest after Luke Wilding's death?' Andrew asked.

73

'There was an inquiry after about three months. Not an actual inquest. It was simply opened and closed.'

'Do you think they still believe they'll ever find the man who did it?'

'I doubt if they ever close their file on a murder.'

'That man Ross—I believe he's the man who's here today, isn't he?—has kept harassing Jan about it, so she said.'

'He has,' Clare said. 'She's told me about it. And now the way she's disappeared today isn't going to help her. I wish she hadn't done it.'

'Then you think she went voluntarily,' Andrew said.

'Don't you?'

'I'd have thought if she was able to do that she'd have come down to the rest of us on the beach. Why d'you think she went off by herself?'

The two Nicholls exchanged glances, then David said hesitantly, 'It's just that she's always been afraid the police are going to frame her sooner or later for Luke Wilding's murder. I don't think there's any risk of anything like that myself, but you can't get her to talk reasonably about it. And if she came on Kay's body, but hadn't seen the actual murder happen, I think she might have jumped to the conclusion that she'd be suspected and lost her head and bolted.'

'Tony doesn't think that,' Andrew said. 'He thinks she was forced to leave.'

'Perhaps he's right.'

'Is it possible the murder could have been done in the house without her knowing it?' Andrew asked.

'Oh yes, I think so,' David said. 'We know she changed into her bathers, don't we? Well, if she'd been in the bedroom, changing, with the door shut, and someone came quietly into the house—after all, the front door wasn't locked and anyone who knew the Lightfoots would have known it probably wouldn't be at that time of day—so someone could have come in and taken Kay by surprise in the lounge, knocked her unconscious before she'd time to scream, finished the job of killing her and made off without Jan hearing a thing.'

Andrew nodded thoughtfully. 'I suppose it's possible. But this person who came in . . .'

'Yes?'

'You think it's someone who knew the Lightfoots well, someone who knew the door wouldn't be locked and knew she was in the house, in other words, very likely someone in this room?'

David shook his head. 'We aren't the only people who'd know a thing like that. They'd lots of friends—I mean, acquaintances, people they'd often entertained here. They led a very social sort of life. Denis being Director of the Institute, they seemed to think that was part of the job.'

'So you think Kay had a relationship with one of those people which no one else knew about, which made that person hate her so much that he came here to kill her at a time when there was actually someone else in the house. Isn't it more likely that some vagrant had seen us all go down to the beach, thought the house was empty, came in to see what he could pick up, was taken by surprise by Kay and killed her?'

'Yes,' Clare said. 'Yes, I'm sure that's how it was. It couldn't have been any of us here. I'm sure Andrew's right, David.'

'But if it had happened like that,' David said, 'I mean if Kay took him by surprise and not the other way round, she'd have had time to scream, wouldn't she, and Jan would have heard her? So it doesn't help us to guess how or why Jan's vanished.'

'But at least it suggests a motive for Kay's murder,' Andrew said.

'Mr Nicholl,' a uniformed constable interrupted them, 'Sergeant Ross would like a few words with you in the other room.'

David got up and left them. Clare was the next to be questioned. Andrew, as he had guessed he would be, was the last. Just before he was summoned to the study he glanced at his watch. The time was nearly two o'clock in the morning. The house was no longer so full of people. Most of them had finished the work that they had come there to do. Kay's body had been taken away to the morgue. The piece of crystal on which Kay's blood had dried had been wrapped up in a sheet of plastic and removed with the care of something precious.

Andrew was very tired. It occurred to him as he waited for his turn to meet Sergeant Ross that he had not really stopped feeling tired since he had left Heathrow. It had taken him at least two days to recover from the journey, then there had been the difficulty of adjusting to the ten hours' difference in time, and then there had been the fact that, much as he had enjoyed the sunshine and the swimming, the ninety degrees was surprisingly exhausting. As he was led by the constable to the study he caught himself giving a deep yawn and hoping that the sergeant would not keep him long.

Sergeant Ross saw the yawn, let his crooked mouth tilt up in his sardonic smile and said, 'Tired, Professor?'

'A little,' Andrew admitted.

'Well, sit down. We'll try not to keep you long. You're here on a holiday, I believe.'

The sergeant was sitting at a desk on which there was a litter of papers which Andrew supposed belonged to Denis and that had been thrust aside. Andrew took a chair facing the sergeant across the desk.

'Yes,' he said.

'Ever been in Australia before?'

'Once, for a short time.'

'When was that?'

'About four years ago. I'd just retired and I took a trip

round the world to celebrate, so to speak, doing some lecturing here and there.'

'You came to Adelaide?'

'Yes.'

'Why was that?'

'I'd been invited to lecture at the university.'

'It wasn't to see Dr Gardiner?'

'He was working at Canberra at that time. I did go there to see him.'

'You've known him for some time, then.'

'Yes, he was a student of mine in London when he was working for his Ph.D. and we've always kept in touch.'

'He wasn't married when you were here before?'

'No.'

'How long have you known his wife and her sister?'

Andrew had a feeling that it was only then that the sergeant's questioning really began. Until then he had only been feeling his way, trying to find some point at which he might make contact with Andrew.

'I've known Mrs Gardiner since last Thursday, when I arrived,' he said. 'I met Mrs Lightfoot for the first time this morning.'

Sergeant Ross took his long chin in his hand and tugged at it thoughtfully.

'Does anything occur to you,' he said, 'has anything struck you about the relationships of the people you've met here today, which could have any bearing on what's happened?'

'So you think it's one of them who's probably guilty,' Andrew said. 'Not some outsider who came in here by chance.'

'I wouldn't go so far as to say that,' the sergeant said. 'But there was another murder about a year ago which most of the same people were involved in. Have you heard about that?'

'Yes, I've been told about it.'

'And it doesn't suggest anything to you?'

'Nothing at all.'

'The victim then was Mrs Gardiner's first husband. She hadn't any alibi, but the body was moved a considerable distance after the murder and she couldn't have done that unless she had an accomplice. She had a motive, of course. Wilding maltreated her and he left her a good deal of money. Another person who had a motive was his son, Robert. He inherited his father's sheep station and a good deal of money. But he had an alibi. He'd gone out for the day with Mrs Lightfoot—Miss Ramsden as she was then—who hadn't married Lightfoot yet and who was thought by some people, mistakenly, I believe, to be having an affair with young Wilding. If they weren't mistaken and she and Wilding were thinking of getting married, you could say she'd got a motive too. Then if Gardiner was already in love with Janet Wilding and thought she'd marry him if old Wilding could be got out of the way, and liked the idea of a wife with money, he'd a motive also. And Nicholl was the person who found the body. I don't know of any motive he might have had for murdering Wilding, but it would actually have been easier for him to have done the murder than anyone else. He'd a habit of going to that quarry, hunting for crystal, malachite and so on, and he could easily have done the murder and dragged the body down to the pond, then given the alarm that he'd just found it. And his wife, if she knew about it, would naturally have kept quiet.'

'I don't understand,' Andrew said. 'Why are you going into all this? Isn't it Mrs Lightfoot's murder you're investigating at the moment, not Luke Wilding's?'

'You don't see the point?'

'I can't say I do.'

Sergeant Ross gave an unhappy sigh. 'Maybe I'm obsessed,' he said. 'I've been told I am, but I mean to get the man who murdered Luke Wilding before I'm finished. And I was just pointing out to you that everyone who's here today was somehow involved in the Wilding killing. If we can solve who did the murder today, perhaps we'll have the solution to the other murder.'

'Was Miss Massingham involved in the Wilding murder?' Andrew asked. 'You haven't mentioned her.'

'Perhaps you don't know she's had an affair going for some time with Robert Wilding,' Ross said. 'And she may like money as much as most people.'

'Who told you about that?' Andrew asked.

'Nobody here, but I've had my eye on this group of people ever since Wilding's murder and there isn't much about them I don't know.'

'I believe his murder matters to you more than Mrs Lightfoot's,' Andrew said.

'Didn't I tell you I'm obsessed?' Ross was pulling at his chin again. 'Maybe it's just that I've been told so often I'll never solve it. I don't like being told I'll never do a thing. I don't like being defeated. But let's go back to Mrs Lightfoot. The fact is, I just wanted to make sure you knew the background of all these people you've met here today and then I wanted to ask you again if anything's struck you about them that might cast light on the murder.'

'All I can say is that it was a particularly pleasant day until the murder,' Andrew said. 'I found everyone very likeable. The food and drink were excellent. I had two very enjoyable swims and a very restful doze on the beach. In a way, since the shock of discovering the murder, it's difficult to remember how pleasant it all was. But in fact I haven't spent such a delightful Christmas Day for a long time.'

'You didn't sense any—uneasiness, any tension—between any two people?'

Andrew decided to say nothing about the tension that he had thought since his arrival existed between Tony and Jan.

'No,' he said.

'Then let's get back to that doze of yours,' Ross said. 'And those two swims. Were all the rest of the party down on the beach with you?'

'I think so, except of course Mrs Lightfoot and Mrs Gardiner.'

'Yes, except them.'

'And except for the time when I was asleep. I don't know where they all were then.'

'You were really asleep?'

'Dead to the world.'

'So that during that time anyone could have come and gone without your knowing anything about it?'

'Easily.'

'But when you went in swimming, what about then?'

Andrew put an elbow on the desk in front of him, leant his head on his hand and tried to concentrate. It would have been easier if he had not been so tired. But he wanted to help the sergeant. He thought his questions perfectly reasonable. Only to remember what had happened in the afternoon between the massive Christmas dinner and the discovery of the murder seemed extraordinarily difficult. A kind of fog clouded his brain.

'I think the way it happened,' he said, 'is that when we first went down to the beach we all went in to swim. But as you know, you have to go a long way before the water gets deep enough for you to be able to swim properly. After a bit I just struck out into it and so did Wilding—yes, I think it was Wilding, but it might have been one of the others or even some stranger—he swam past me, but I didn't pay much attention to him or to what any of the others were doing. I was quite alone out there for a while. Then I swam in again, settled down on the beach and went to sleep.'

'You didn't happen to notice a bright green towel on the beach before you went to sleep?'

'No.'

'Right. Go on.'

'Well, I saw Miss Massingham under the umbrella thing

they'd brought down to the beach with them. And Nicholl and his wife were in the shallow water, near the shore. And after a time I decided to swim again, and when I'd got out some way I met Gardiner, swimming in. He said it was time to be going back to the house and went on past me. I swam about for a bit, then Lightfoot and Wilding, who'd been farther out, came by and we all went in. And it was then that Gardiner noticed the towel.'

'The towel,' Sergeant Ross said, 'is a problem.'

'I can see it must be if you've made up your mind Mrs Gardiner killed her sister,' Andrew said.

'I haven't made up my mind about anything.' There was bitterness in the sergeant's voice, as if it offended him to have an error of the kind attributed to him. 'I've got what's usually called a completely open mind, though you might also call it a bloody blank one. But it's her towel. Her husband's sure of that. There's a tear on the fringe of it which he remembers having made himself some weeks ago. And it's got blood on it and it was taken down to the beach and dropped there. And Mrs Gardiner, in her bathers, seems to have taken off in the opposite direction. That's to say, she seems to have gone home and driven off God knows where. There's a call out for the car, but nothing's come in yet. It doesn't make much sense, as far as we've got.'

'About that towel . . .'

'Yes?' The sergeant's gaze sharpened as if he thought, from Andrew's tone of voice, that at last he was about to tell him something useful.

'Do you know anything about a young Englishman called Dudley Blair?' Andrew asked.

'Blair?' Ross said it in a tone so extremely vague that Andrew immediately felt certain that he knew the name quite well. 'Rings a bell, somehow.'

'He seems to be a sort of drop-out,' Andrew said, 'who happens to be a gifted silversmith whose things are sold by Miss Massingham in her shop. And he's a friend of the

Gardiners and on my first night here in Betty Hill he came in and borrowed a towel. It was a bright green towel, just like the one Gardiner found on the beach and thought was his wife's. If it wasn't, is it possible it was dropped there by Blair?'

'Ah, if it wasn't . . .' The sergeant suddenly smiled with both corners of his mouth, not merely with the sardonic tilting of one side of it. 'Thank you, Professor, that's very useful. It opens up all kinds of possibilities.'

After that he let Andrew go, almost as if he was all at once in a hurry to get rid of him.

It was three o'clock before Andrew and Tony drove back to the Gardiners' bungalow. The night sky was clear and the stars were brilliant. The Southern Cross shone low above the horizon. Tony was silent and Andrew felt no inclination to probe into the anxieties that seemed to have raised a wall between the two of them. From the expression on Tony's face he might have been unaware that there was anyone sitting beside him. He drove more recklessly than usual and even when he swung the car in at his gate and stopped in front of the door, he still said nothing.

They went into the house and Tony left the door behind him standing open. Frowning, withdrawn and ignoring Andrew, he went quickly from room to room, then out to the garage. Andrew, who meanwhile had gone to the living-room and was standing at a window, looking out into the dark garden, saw that he did not put the car away.

By then Andrew had reached the stage of weariness when he no longer wanted to go to bed. There was no hope that he would sleep if he did. He would only toss and fret and soon get up again and start wandering restlessly about the house. He began longing for the dawn. Once daylight was back, he thought, it would be possible to cancel out, as it were, this dreadful night and start the business of normal living again.

Not that it really would be. But at the moment he could almost convince himself that morning would bring back everyday life, with some good strong coffee for breakfast, and with luck, if he could find it, a small piece of cheese. He always found it difficult to believe that a day had really begun till he had had some cheese. What had begun as a dietetic experiment in which he had not had much faith had become almost an addiction.

He was thinking about this and wondering if it might not be a good idea to make some breakfast now since Jan was not there to do it when it suddenly occurred to him that Tony was still moving rapidly about the house. He heard the slam of a cupboard door, then in another room a drawer being opened and violently closed, then what sounded like a kettle being filled at the kitchen sink, then an outburst of swearing. A moment later Andrew heard coffee being ground in the electric grinder. So Tony was making coffee. That was very satisfactory. Andrew went to the kitchen. There was bread, butter and some boiled ham on the table and it looked as if Tony had started to make some sandwiches.

'Can I help?' Andrew asked.

'Why don't you go to bed?' Tony said.

'I don't feel much like it.'

'You look flat out.'

'I'm all right.' As he said it Andrew's eyes fell on a suitcase on one of the kitchen chairs. 'Going somewhere?' he inquired.

'That's the idea.' Tony slammed some ham on to a slice of bread, clapping another slice on top of it, then took a large bite out of the resulting sandwich. 'Help yourself,' he said. 'I'm just making some coffee, then I'll be off.'

'Where are you going?' Andrew asked.

'Looking for Jan, of course.'

'Do you know where she is?'

83

'I've a pretty good idea. I looked around here to make sure she hadn't come home after that cop came looking for her, and I looked in the garage to make sure the Volvo's gone, and since it has and since she isn't here, I can make a fair guess at where she probably is.'

'You told me, and I believe the sergeant too, that you didn't know.'

'So I did.'

'Wasn't that a mistake?'

'Why should it be? She'd her reasons for doing what she did. I don't want to get in her way.'

'But they'll catch up with her sooner or later and then it isn't going to help her that you've obstructed them.'

'I'm not obstructing them, and as it happens at the moment, I'm only making a guess. If I find her I may try to persuade her to give herself up to them.'

The kettle began to whistle. Tony poured the boiling water into a coffee filter and the fragrance of it filled the kitchen. While he was doing it Andrew made himself a ham sandwich.

'You don't want to tell me where you're going, then,' he said.

'As a matter of fact . . .' Tony paused and seemed to be giving all his attention to the dripping of the coffee through the filter. 'As a matter of fact, I was thinking of asking you if you'd feel like coming with me, but I guess you're too tired. You need a rest.'

'If you'd tell me where you're going . . .'

'To Hartwell, of course. When Jan's in trouble, she goes to her father. She's always done that. And he still lives there.'

'How long does it take to get there?'

'A couple of hours.'

'So if you're right that that's where she's gone, she'll have got there by now.'

'That's for sure.'

'So why don't you telephone and ask if she's there? It might save you a wasted journey.'

Tony brought the coffee-pot and two cups to the table and poured out the coffee.

'The old man's deaf as a post. He's got a telephone, but he never uses it. Half-blind also, but amazingly independent. Lives alone and won't have anyone to help him. And I don't think there's much risk the journey's going to be wasted. As I said, when Jan's in trouble, she goes straight to him. And apart from the trouble she's in, she'll have thought someone's got to break the news to him about Kay's death. He was never very fond of Kay as far as I could see. For some reason they always got across each other. But after all, she was his daughter.'

Andrew sipped some coffee, then bit into his sandwich. After a moment he said, 'Do you really want me to go with you, Tony?'

'Well, you might be a help,' Tony answered. 'We could talk the thing over and you might stop me running away with some crazy ideas I've got. The idea, for instance, of what it'll mean if we don't find Jan at Hartwell. She's there, I'm sure, but just suppose she isn't . . . Andrew, I can't bear to think of it.'

'All right, let's go,' Andrew said. 'Just let me finish this sandwich.'

CHAPTER 5

The road was steep with one bend after another and Tony's driving that night was terrifying. He swung round corner after corner in a way that shook Andrew from side to side in his seat. As they climbed they saw the whole city of Adelaide spread out beneath them, a shining pattern of lights printed on the darkness, all in rectangles. There can be few cities in the world where the planning of its streets has so meticulously avoided any curve. The main streets were wide, straight lines bisected at intervals by other wide, straight lines, the spaces between them filled by other narrower straight lines, all of them a-glitter.

Their brilliance in the clear air seemed strange to Andrew, accustomed as he was to the way the lights of London are softened by the London atmosphere. But soon the sparkling outlines of the city vanished, as the car swooped round a bend and dived between hills. There was a full moon in the sky and he could dimly see their shapes. He did his best to relax and not let himself be too scared by Tony's driving.

Tony had said that he would be glad of a chance to talk to Andrew, among other things of what it might mean if they did not find Jan at Hartwell. But now he showed no sign of wanting to talk. He sat crouched over the wheel, scowling at the road ahead of him. Andrew had never seen the expression on his face that he saw there now. He had never seen it other than open, candid and friendly. But now it was withdrawn and hard. It made Andrew wonder what it meant to Tony that Jan should have gone in her trouble, if he really believed that she had, to her father rather than to him.

Andrew snatched a little sleep as they drove on. The road had become dead straight and level and he succeeded in dozing for brief spells from time to time. Dawn came before they reached the end of the journey. The moon disappeared, the sky grew softly grey, then presently a line of flame appeared along the horizon. They were driving across a great plain edged in the far distance by mountains and covered by a ragged mass of mallee, a straggly, angular kind of scrub. The road was still a narrow straight line across it. There was no other traffic. Tony had lost the look almost of ferocity with which he had started the drive and now looked only tired and lost.

It was he who at last broke the silence as the road dipped,

then curved, then passed a few buildings which appeared to be on the outer edge of a small township.

'If Jan isn't here, I shan't know what to do,' he said.

'What will you do if she is?' Andrew asked.

'Try to find out what made her run away. But it may be no good. There are things she won't talk about.'

'Will you try to get her to go back with you?'

'That may be no good either. She had her reasons for coming and if the reasons seem good enough I shan't try to make her do anything she doesn't want to. It wouldn't work, anyway. She's stubborn, you know. She looks such a fragile little thing, but there's steel somewhere inside her. I've known her for a long time and I think I understand her pretty well.'

'Tony, do you really believe you're going to find her, or do you believe what you said at first, that someone made her leave and may have driven away with her in the Volvo?' Andrew did not end the sentence in the way that he did in his thoughts: '. . . and may have killed her?'

Tony drew his breath in sharply in a sound that was almost a sob. 'We're going to find her. Once I'd thought of her coming to her father, I knew the other idea had been just a nightmare. Of course we'll find her.'

Andrew nodded as if he had no doubts of it himself.

Tony went on, 'Tell me something, Andrew. We know each other pretty well. Do you think I'm capable of committing a murder?'

'It would surprise me very much if you were,' Andrew said.

'But you don't think it's impossible.'

'Impossible is a big word. I don't know what I might possibly do myself, given the circumstances. But I don't believe I could kill anyone in cold blood. It would have to be hot blood and I'm not sure how much I've got in my system.'

'So you think I might have killed Luke.'

Andrew was startled. 'For God's sake, Tony, I didn't say that.'

'All the same, given the circumstances, you think I could have done it. And then, because Kay had found it out, I could have killed her. Don't you see, I'm trying to think out why Jan's frightened of me. Because if she did leave home of her own free will, and not because she'd a gun at her back, that must be why she left, mustn't it? She thinks she's got herself married to a murderer.'

'I don't believe it for a moment,' Andrew said.

'It's what the police believe. And they believe it's why we got married so indecently soon after Luke's death. They think it's so that she hasn't got to give evidence against me.'

'Incidentally, why did you get married so quickly?' Andrew asked. 'You might have been wiser to let it wait for a while.'

'For the simple reason that we were in love with one another, though we only found it out after she'd got married.'

'I think you're getting confused, Tony,' Andrew said. 'If she married you, believing you'd murdered Luke, then she isn't frightened of murder as such, so she's no reason to run away from you. And if she knows you didn't murder him, then she's no reason at all to be frightened of you.'

They had been passing houses, most of them bungalows with roofs of corrugated iron and narrow verandahs built around them. They stood in biggish patches of land, some of them surrounded with what looked like market gardens, filled with straight rows of vegetables, or vines and olive trees. There were tall trees too dotted here and there between them. Presently the road became a street with shops, still closed, on either side of it, and one or two inns, all still and silent, a school and a church. They drove on till the houses began to thin again, then Tony swung the car to the left up a stony drive and stopped in front of one of the iron-roofed bungalows.

'The old man may not be up yet,' he said as he got out

of the car, 'and if he isn't, I don't know if we'll be able to wake him. I told you he's very deaf, didn't I?'

'But if Jan's here, she'll hear us,' Andrew said.

'Yes—yes, of course.' But for the first time it sounded as if Tony really doubted that he would find her.

The small house looked neglected and almost as if it might be empty. The paint on the door had been flaking away. There were weeds thrusting their way between the two or three steps that led up to it. A large cobweb had draped itself from one of the verandah supports to the roof. The garden looked as if it were a long time since it had received any attention.

Tony went up to the door and hammered on it with a rusty knocker.

There was no reply and after a moment he knocked again.

This time there was a sound of footsteps inside, slow, slithering footsteps that sounded as if they were made by someone in loose slippers. But then these stopped and there was silence again. It seemed to Andrew that there must be someone inside who was waiting and listening.

Tony knocked again, more violently.

The slow tread inside came nearer, then the door was opened a few inches and an old, wrinkled face appeared in the opening. Then the door was flung wide and a voice that grated hoarsely ejaculated, 'Would you believe it—Tony!'

Andrew's first impression of the man in the doorway was that he was very old. Too old to be the father of young women like Kay Lightfoot and Jan Gardiner. But then Andrew realized that the man after all was probably younger than he was himself. But his tall body was very emaciated, with the skin that covered it drawn tightly over the skeleton inside and deeply wrinkled over the strong bones of the face. It was tanned a yellowish brown in which the grey eyes looked very pale and a little cloudy. He had a hearing aid in one ear, with a flex dangling from it, leading to a battery in the pocket of the stained blue shirt he was wearing. He had on crumpled cotton shorts that hung low on his hips and checked felt slippers. His legs were very lean and hairy. The hair on them was grey, like the uncombed mop that stood up from his forehead.

'Tony,' he said again. 'Well, well, what d'you know?'

As he said it, his hand went to the battery in his shirt pocket to switch it on.

'Is Jan here?' Tony asked, raising his voice so that the deaf man could hear him.

'No, why should she be?' the other man asked.

'I don't believe it,' Tony said. 'I think she's here.'

'What's the trouble? You two been falling out, or something?'

'No,' Tony said with desperation in his voice. 'No, I just think she's here.'

'Now why should you have got that idea into your head?' The man, whom Andrew could not stop himself thinking of as aged, worn and tired, stood to one side so that Tony and Andrew could enter the house. 'Who's your friend?' he inquired.

'I'm sorry—this is Professor Basnett,' Tony said. 'I was a student of his in London. He's on a visit to us in Betty Hill. Andrew, this is my father-in-law.'

'My name's Sam Ramsden.' The man thrust out a hand. 'Glad to know you, Professor. I've heard Tony talk about you. Now what's eating you, Tony? What's happened?'

'You mean you don't know about what's happened to Kay?' Tony demanded.

'I don't know a thing. How could I?'

'But you were expecting me this morning. Me or someone. Perhaps the police.'

'I don't have much dealings with the police,' Sam Ramsden said. 'I have a couple of grogs now and then with Bill Peters, our constable, but that's all and I wouldn't expect him to drop in on me at this hour of the morning.'

'Then why didn't you come straight to the door and open

it when I knocked?' Tony asked. 'You took a long time making up your mind whether or not to do it.'

The same thought had occurred to Andrew. He remembered the sound of caution about the slippered feet inside the door before it was opened.

'I came straight enough,' Sam Ramsden answered. 'I wasn't expecting anyone. Took me by surprise. Wasn't even sure I'd heard correctly.' He touched the battery in his shirt pocket. 'I hadn't got this switched on. Seemed unlikely it was visitors.'

'It wasn't to give Jan time to hide?'

Her father gave a helpless shake of his head. 'Why would she want to hide from you, even supposing she was here? You've got your wires crossed, Tony, that's for sure. Now come in and I'll get you some tea. And some bacon and eggs—how about that? Or a bit of steak. I've got a nice bit of steak somewhere. How would you feel about a nice bit of steak, Professor, with a fried egg on top of it?'

Andrew had heard about this hearty form of Australian breakfast, though he had never had to face it.

'Some tea would be fine,' he said, then remembered that he ought to raise his voice. But he knew that he need not raise it much. Years of lecturing had given him a voice that carried without his having to make much effort. 'I'm not very hungry. Though if you happened to have some cheese —but please don't go to any trouble.'

'Bread and cheese? No trouble at all, though it's not my idea of a breakfast. And what about you, Tony? Steak and an egg?'

'No, thank you, just tea,' Tony answered. 'I'm not hungry either. Dad, is it true you haven't heard about Kay?'

They had gone along a narrow passage into a disorderly kitchen. It looked as if it were where Tony's father-in-law spent most of his time. Besides unwashed dishes in the sink, there were newspapers and a few books heaped on the table with an ashtray full of stubs amongst them, an easy chair with wooden arms and worn cushions in one corner and a television set facing it.

Going to a refrigerator, Sam Ramsden opened it and started searching about in its jumbled contents.

'Cheese,' he muttered. 'Cheese—yes, here we are. Kay, you said. Something about Kay. What was that?'

Tony was looking at him with a frown of uncertainty and some bewilderment on his face. It was plain that events were not turning out as he had expected. Then suddenly his gaze sharpened.

'Taken up smoking again?' he asked. 'I thought you'd given it up.'

'So I have. Why d'you ask? Oh—' Sam Ramsden saw that Tony was looking at the stubs in the ashtray. 'I see, no, those weren't mine. Can't afford to smoke these days. But a mate of mine was in here yesterday evening, chain-smoker, God knows where he gets the money for it. Myself, I've got so I don't even like the smell of it any more, but I don't interfere with other people's pleasures.'

'That mate wasn't Jan?' Tony asked. 'She's getting on for a chain-smoker.'

'Jan? I thought we were talking about Kay.' Sam Ramsden plugged in the electric kettle, made some room on the table by bundling books and newspapers on to a chair, and brought mugs out of a cupboard.

Tony's face was very troubled as he looked at the older man. 'You really don't know what's happened, Dad?'

'I don't know anything. Don't tell me she's left her husband or anything crazy like that. Denis is a good chap.'

'No. If you really don't know, then—well, she's dead.'

It was not perhaps the best way of breaking bad news to a parent, though Andrew was inclined to believe that when bad news had to be broken, and he had been on the receiving end of it several times in his life, there was a certain virtue in making the blow come hard and quickly. The apprehension that could build up inside you while tactful words were being sought with which to soften the pain of the blow could be as hurtful as the shock of being told the stark truth all at once.

Sam Ramsden, who had been at the cupboard from which he had taken the mugs and was just taking a bag of sugar out of it, became quite still. His back was to Tony and Andrew and neither of them could see his face. But after a moment he turned. There had been no change of expression on it.

'Dead?' he said. 'How did that happen? Car accident?' There was not even a tremor in his hoarse voice.

Tony threw himself down in a chair, leant his elbows on the table and took his face in his hands.

'Look, if I've got things wrong, I'm sorry,' he said. 'I thought for sure you knew Kay was killed, murdered, yesterday afternoon. We'd had our Christmas dinner with her and Denis—Jan, Andrew and I and a few other people—and after it all we went down to the beach for a swim except for Kay and Jan who stayed behind to clear up, and we didn't get back to the house till early evening. But when we did we found Kay . . .'

He paused, giving his father-in-law a look of acute distress. He had just poured some boiling water into the teapot. The hand that held the kettle was quite steady.

'She was in the lounge,' Tony went on, 'and she was dead. Her head had been battered in with that lump of crystal I gave her and Denis. There was a lot of blood. It was—horrible. And Jan was gone.'

'What d'you mean, gone?' Sam Ramsden said. He drew a chair up to the table and gestured to Andrew to do the same. 'Where did she go?'

'That's what I came here to find out,' Tony answered. 'I thought she must have come here.'

The other man gave a slow shake of his head. 'Why'd she do that?'

'She's always come to you when she's been in trouble.'

'No, it was Kay she always went to. I couldn't manage her myself, but she'd do anything Kay told her. Great friends they were, specially as kids. Jan always trailed around after Kay, not a bit jealous because, as everyone said, Kay was the pretty one. She was that, but she never had any sense. I knew she'd get into bad trouble sooner or later. And now it's happened. Can't say I exactly expected it, the way you've described it. I used to think she'd make trouble for other people, leading them on, then letting them down. She was fond of doing that, and one day, I thought, she'd go too far with the wrong chap and have to pay for it. It's what she did with young Wilding, you know. I suppose he isn't under suspicion, by any chance? They were all set to get married when she went off and married Denis.'

'To go by what Wilding told me,' Andrew said, 'he's engaged to another woman and very happy about it. If he wanted revenge on your daughter, he's chosen a strange time for it.'

'So he's engaged, is he?' Sam Ramsden looked about as interested in this piece of information as he had in the story of Kay's death. No sign of grief had appeared on his craggy face. 'And they've no idea who killed the girl? They don't know anything?'

Tony suddenly pounded the table with his fist. 'But where's Jan?' he shouted. 'If she didn't come here, where did she go? She went off in her bathers, leaving her clothes behind, and she went home and took the Volvo and disappeared. If she didn't come to you, then someone must have made her do that because she saw him murder Kay. And she's probably dead herself by now, with her body dumped somewhere in the bush.'

'It's all right, darling, I'm here,' a soft, rather high-pitched voice said from the doorway. 'You needn't worry about me.'

*

Jan was standing there. At some time she had picked up the red and white cotton dress in which Andrew had seen her first and she had her fair hair tied back in a pony-tail with a scarlet ribbon. Her small, pointed face was very pale and her huge eyes had smears of exhaustion under them. She had a half-smoked cigarette in one hand.

'Thanks, Dad, it was a good try,' she said, coming forward, 'but he'd have found me sooner or later. He'd only got to go round to the back to find the Volvo.' She put a hand on Tony's shoulder. Her touch made him go rigid. There was as much anger as relief on his face. 'I'm sorry, Tony,' she went on. 'I'd have let you know later today where I was if you'd stayed at home. I never thought of you thinking I was dead, or that you'd drive up here right away.'

'And brought the police with him, that's what he'll have done.' Sam Ramsden turned on Tony. 'Didn't you think of that? You don't suppose they let you come here without putting a tail on you. They'll be knocking at the door any time now. Jan, go back into the attic. I'll drive the Volvo out into the bush and leave it somewhere. That's what I was going to do when you and your friend arrived, Tony. That's why I was up so early. We can think what we'll do about it later.'

'It's no good,' Jan said. 'If the police have followed him, they'll find me anyway. Tony—'

He interrupted her by springing to his feet, taking her in his arms and crushing her against him.

'And I thought you were dead!' he exploded. 'How could you do it to me, Jan? If you were frightened, why didn't you come to me? I was down there on the beach. You know I'd have looked after you.'

She withdrew from his embrace with a certain stiffness.

'I lost my head,' she said, but so calmly that it sounded as if it were not a thing that she was in the habit of doing. 'I was scared, I only wanted to get away.'

'But what did you see? Who was it?' He had let her go reluctantly.

She went to the cupboard, took another mug from it and poured out tea for them all.

'I didn't see anything, though I didn't think anyone would believe that,' she said. 'But it's the truth, I don't know anything about it. That's partly why I was so scared. I thought that man Ross would be certain it was me. He's never given up the idea that I killed Luke, or at least that I know who did it, and he kind of hates me because he can't prove it. So if he had a chance to prove I killed Kay, that's what he'd do, even if he didn't really believe it. He'd have thought of it as getting me for Luke's murder.'

'But what happened?' Tony asked. 'You must have seen something. What was it?'

She shook her head. 'Really, I didn't see anything till I found Kay's body. I must have been in the bedroom, changing, when it happened. She and I had cleared up the dining-room and she'd filled the dish-washer and set it going. And it's a pretty noisy one and she'd left the kitchen door open and I think that may have been why I didn't hear anyone come in. And I didn't hurry, because after that great dinner we'd had I didn't feel much like swimming. But then I changed and went to the door and called out to her. She didn't answer, so then I thought she'd got tired of waiting for me and had gone down to the beach without me. It was just chance that I didn't go straight down myself without looking for her. But something made me take a look in the lounge and there she was, lying on the hearthrug with her head . . .' Suddenly the unnaturally calm voice began to shake. 'With her head—oh God! You saw it, Tony, you must have seen it. And that crystal lying beside her, all smeared with blood. The thing looked as if it was bleeding itself. I think I screamed then, and then I ran out to the toilet and was sick, and then—well, I told you, I lost my head. I thought, there I was alone in the house with her

96

and Ross would say I'd done it, and all I could think of was getting away.'

'But why should anyone think you'd done it?' Tony asked. 'You'd nothing against Kay. Everyone knew what good friends you were.'

'A man like Ross wouldn't have listened to what you said about that. He'd have dug up something. Or that's what I thought then. I know I was a fool, I ought to have gone down to the beach and told you what had happened, but what I did was run home as fast as I could. I didn't even wait to change out of my bathers. I only thought of that when I got home. I changed into a dress in a hurry and put a few things in a bag and drove up here. And I told Dad the whole story and he said the best thing would be for me to hide till we knew if the police were coming after me, then think it over quietly and decide what I ought to do.'

It was easy to understand now why Sam Ramsden had been so strangely unmoved by the news of his daughter's murder. He had known almost as much about it as Tony and Andrew themselves. Indeed, perhaps even more, if Jan had spoken more freely to him than she had to Tony.

Andrew had drunk his tea and had found that it relieved his tiredness wonderfully.

'Jan, do you remember what you did with the towel you took to your sister's house in the morning?' he asked. 'A bright green towel.'

She was leaning against the cupboard now, nursing her mug in both hands.

'A towel?' she said. 'I don't remember anything about a towel.'

'You can't remember what towel you took with you?'

'I don't think so . . . Yes, I can. It was one of our green ones. But I didn't take it away with me. I think I dropped it in the lounge, or perhaps in the passage when I found Kay's body and rushed out and was sick. I'd meant to go down to the beach, you see, so I must have had it with me, but I can't remember what I did with it. I know I didn't take it home. Why? Is it important?'

'It's only that Tony found that towel on the beach before we went indoors,' Andrew said, 'and it had bloodstains on it.'

She gazed at him with the blank, unblinking look that he had often seen in her eyes. Then with the pitch of her voice rising even higher than usual, she exclaimed, 'Oh, I see! I think I see! You think I'm lying because that towel was in the bedroom where I changed till I came out to go to the beach, so the murderer must have got it from me to clean himself up, so I must have seen him.'

'He could have picked it up after you'd gone,' Andrew said. 'But it does look as if he may have been in the house still when you found your sister's body. You said you called out to her when you came out of your room. That could have warned him. Is there anywhere he could have hidden till you left the house?'

'Yes, all kinds of places. He could simply have dropped behind the settee, or jumped out of the window and crouched under it, or even slipped behind the door. I didn't look for anyone. I wasn't in a state to notice anything.'

'But weren't you afraid he might still be in the house?'

'I suppose I was, in a way. I was very frightened. But all that made me want to do was to get away. I didn't think it out, but I know I didn't want to come face to face with anyone in the house.'

Tony had sprung up again and grasped her by both arms. He shook her so that the mug that she was holding fell to the ground. A puddle of tea slopped out of it on to the floor.

'But you did see him, didn't you?' Tony yelled at her. 'You know who it was. Why are you shielding him?'

'Let me go!' she shrieked back at him. 'Don't shake me! Don't ever touch me like that! It's what Luke used to do. It's just like Luke!'

As she spat it at Tony and he shamefacedly let her go, the door knocker reverberated through the house.

There was sudden silence in the kitchen. Not only silence, but no one moved. Then the knocker sounded again.

Sam Ramsden got up and shambled towards the door. He could be heard talking to someone there, then he returned, followed by two men. They were in plainclothes, but they could not have been anything but policemen.

'I told you they'd follow you here,' Sam said sourly to Tony. 'They weren't far behind you.'

'I'm sorry to intrude,' one of the men said. He was tall, burly and impassive. 'But Sergeant Ross would be obliged if you'd come back to Adelaide with us, Mrs Gardiner. You're the most important witness in the case.'

'You can't make me go!' she cried. 'I don't know anything!'

'As to that, we could take steps,' the man said. 'But if you'd come of your own free will it would be pleasantest for everyone in the end.'

'He's right, you know, Jan,' Tony said. 'We'll have to go back.' He turned to the man. 'You've no objections, I suppose, if I accompany my wife.'

'No objection at all,' the man answered. 'Matter of fact it'll save us trouble.'

'Come along then, Jan,' Tony said. 'Get your things and let's get going.'

'No,' she said. 'No, I won't. I told you, I don't know anything.'

'You can tell that to Sergeant Ross,' the detective said. 'It's as important for him to know what you don't know as what you do. It all helps to build up a picture.'

'That isn't why he wants me,' she said. 'He's already decided I've killed my sister.'

'Oh, I wouldn't say that,' he answered. 'But perhaps you saw something, heard something, which perhaps you didn't even understand yourself at the time—'

'I didn't!' she broke in. 'All I heard was the dish-washer.'

'Even that could be important, you never know,' he said. 'Now if you're ready . . .'

'Come along, Jan,' Tony said. 'Get your things and let's get moving.' He spoke to the detective again. 'How are we going? D'you want us to drive with you, or in one of our own cars? We've got both of them here. It would be convenient if we could take one of them back to Betty Hill.'

'No objection to your taking one of your own,' the man said.

However, when Jan had jammed the few belongings that she had brought with her into a plastic bag and with a sullen look on her face had gone out to the Holden and Tony had followed her and got into the driver's seat, it turned out that one of the detectives intended to ride with them. Casually, as if he were a passenger whom they had invited to join them, he got into the seat next to Tony and settled himself comfortably. The second man got into the police car and drove down to the road ahead of the car with Tony and Jan in it.

Sam Ramsden, who had gone out on to the verandah with Andrew behind him, turned to him and said, 'Seems as if they somehow forgot about you, Andrew. Now you're stuck here.'

'I'm afraid I rather forgot about myself,' Andrew said. 'It didn't seem to me I was wanted. Is there any way I can get back to Adelaide?'

'You can get back by plane from Hartwell, but not till later in the day. It's too late now for the early plane. Anyway, you look as if you could do with a kip. Come inside and have some more tea and we'll talk over what it's best to do.'

Andrew thought that there was nothing he would have liked so much then as a kip, but he said, 'Can I get a taxi to the airport, if there's one at Hartwell? I don't want to be any trouble to you, Mr Ramsden.'

'My name's Sam,' the other man said. 'And it's no trouble. But I've been thinking . . .'

He paused as he turned and led the way indoors. Andrew followed him in. They returned to the kitchen and Sam Ramsden poured away the cooling tea and started to make some more. Andrew sat down again at the table.

'I've been thinking, we might drive down to Adelaide ourselves,' Sam went on. 'I'm thinking of Denis. I ought to go and see if there's anything I can do for him. I always liked him, though I never thought he and Kay would hit it off together. He's a quiet sort of chap, wrapped up in his work, and she's pretty lively. But she liked the idea of living in the city and with Denis being head of that marine biology place, I suppose it made her feel kind of important. I'd never managed to give the girls much of a life here.' He looked vaguely round the kitchen, at the unwashed dishes, the old newspapers, the dust that had accumulated everywhere. 'But it's worse now than when they were here to look after things. I've let it all go to pieces. I could get a woman in to clean up for me perhaps. That's what they say I should do. You can sometimes get a Greek or an Italian who'll come. There are a good many immigrants in Hartwell and they're sometimes glad of a job. But I don't like a stranger around the place, that's the truth, and I manage well enough to please myself. Where d'you live, Andrew? London?'

'Yes,' Andrew said.

'I was in London for a while at the beginning of the last war,' Sam said. The kettle was singing again and he put several teaspoonfuls of tea into the teapot. 'I remember a sight I saw. A man was standing in the gutter, playing a fiddle, with a cap on the ground beside him and people dropped pennies into it now and then. Then a Maori soldier came along and he just took the fellow's fiddle away from him and began to play. I don't suppose he played any better than the other chap, but the sight of him, his dark skin and the unfamiliar sort of features he had and his New Zealand uniform, fascinated people and they started crowding round and encouraging him and dropping a shower of pennies into the cap. Then after a little this chap just gave the fiddle back to the other fellow and walked on.' He poured the boiling water into the teapot. 'It was a long time ago. I was quite a young chap, but somehow I've never forgotten it. After that I was in Burma, which wasn't the best time of my life. But I'll tell you something funny about this country. Gallipoli, which happened before most of the people alive now were born, still means more to most of them than anything that happened in the last war.'

Andrew nodded. 'I know that.'

Sam sat down again at the table. He gave the tea a little time to infuse before pouring it out.

'Now we've got to decide what to do,' he said. 'What d'you say to having a bit of a rest now, then driving down with me into Adelaide? There's no hurry. We can take our time. To tell the truth, I'm a slow driver. My eyesight isn't what it was. Quite safe, you understand, but I like to go carefully. But my guess is they'll be keeping Jan and Tony at Headquarters in Adelaide for most of the day, so if we get to Betty Hill by some time in the afternoon it'll be soon enough. But I'd like to see Denis. They'll be giving him a bad time, I reckon—I mean, the press and all—and perhaps I can help. But if you'd sooner go by plane, I'll drive you over to the airport in time for it. The flight only takes twenty minutes or thereabouts.'

'I'll drive with you, if I may,' Andrew said. He had taken a liking to the gaunt man with his harsh voice, his thin, hairy legs and his evident kindliness. There was no resemblance between him and his daughters. His features were coarse compared with theirs and it was obvious that he had had far less education than they had. But behind some roughness in his manner there was a gentleness that was very appealing.

It was in the early afternoon that they started towards

Adelaide. Andrew had spent most of the morning asleep. After he and Sam had drunk their tea Sam had taken him to a small bedroom that clearly was very seldom used. There was a pile of folded blankets on the bed and a pillow covered in dusty striped ticking, and there were a good many cobwebs in the corners of the room. Sam seemed a little surprised at the state that it was in, as if he had not been into it for some time, and apologized for it with some embarrassment. But Andrew would have been ready to sleep on the floor if nothing else had been available. He kicked off his shoes and socks, took off the pale grey tropical suit which he had put on an untold age ago to go to the Lightfoots' Christmas dinner, and threw himself down on the bed. Almost at once he fell into a deep sleep.

He was woken by Sam about one o'clock and told that there was some cold meat and a salad ready, and beer if he felt like it. Sam also offered him the loan of a razor. Andrew shaved, had a sketchy wash, dressed and ate the cold lamb and drank the beer. They set off on the road to Adelaide in the Volvo.

'It's the easiest way to get it back to them,' Sam said. 'I can come back by plane.'

He had packed a small suitcase, so it seemed that he did not intend to return to Hartwell that day.

As he had told Andrew, he drove very carefully. The probability was, Andrew thought, that with his eyesight as it was he ought not to have been driving at all, and his caution communicated itself to Andrew, so that after a little while he found himself feeling almost as nervous as he had at Tony's wild driving the night before. They soon left the fertile area of Hartwell behind them and started across the scrubby plain of mallee. The day was very hot, far hotter than it had been during the last few days in Betty Hill, and the sky was of the deep, intense blue which still filled Andrew with a dreamlike sense of unreality. He wished that, like his host, he was only in a shirt and shorts, instead of his grey suit, and after a short time he took off his jacket and tossed it on to the back seat of the car.

Sam grunted, 'I wondered how soon you'd do that. I suppose in England you're more formal than we are.'

'Perhaps,' Andrew said. 'At least at my age. I don't think you can say it of the young. They seem to be pretty much the same everywhere. Sam, there's something I want to ask you, if you don't mind.'

'All right, give it a go,' Sam invited.

'It's about the way you talk of Kay. You said you always expected her to get into trouble. You didn't think she'd make a success of her marriage. Forgive me if I'm asking what I shouldn't, but what did you think was the matter with her?'

'She was greedy, she was ambitious, she was unscrupulous,' Sam replied bluntly. 'Does that answer what you wanted to know?'

'Yes,' Andrew said, 'fairly completely.'

'And you think it's a stinking way for a father to talk of a daughter who's just been murdered.'

'It does surprise me.'

'All right, then. Forget I said it. The fact is, I loved the girl all the same, though it was quite a strain to keep on doing that once I'd begun to understand her. But I felt maybe it was my own fault. It isn't an easy job for a father to bring up two motherless girls and I guess I made a mess of it.'

'But you wouldn't think it unlikely that Kay may have had enemies.'

'Seems obvious she did, doesn't it?'

'Unless we fall back on the theory of the intruder who didn't know there was anyone in the house, and sometimes that seems the most reasonable explanation.'

Sam shot Andrew a sidelong glance. As a result of it the car swerved abruptly, but fortunately righted itself again. Concentrating on the road ahead of him, Sam was silent for a little while, then he said, 'You don't believe that.'

'I don't know what to believe,' Andrew answered. 'I'm a stranger here. It would be best, I think, if I tried to control my curiosity about what happened.'

'That's right. Don't ask questions. Don't puzzle your brains about it. Leave it to the police. That's what I'm going to do. Now let's turn in here.'

They had reached a gateway at the side of the road over which there was an arch with a big sign on it, 'Calthorpe's Winery'. Sam swung the car in at the gate and drove on along a narrow drive towards some buildings a few hundred yards from the entrance. When they reached these, Andrew saw that they consisted of a bungalow beyond which there was an assemblage of great cylindrical tanks, in which, he assumed, wine was maturing. A notice beside the door of the bungalow, with an arrow on it, said, 'Toilets'. No doubt, if he wanted to make use of these later, he thought, he would find them labelled 'Ladies' and 'Men', which he had noticed before was customary in this country and ought to have told him something about prevalent social attitudes.

'We'll pick up some bottles for Denis,' Sam said as he stopped the car at the entrance to the bungalow. 'No point in arriving empty-handed.'

He led the way into the building. Inside, there was a fair-sized room with a bar along one side of it behind which a woman stood, pouring a few spoonfuls of some wine into several glasses, which she then pushed towards some customers standing at the bar.

'We'll try their white Burgundy,' Sam said as he went to the bar. 'Calthorpe's is pretty good. It's better than their Shiraz, though we can try that too and see if you like it. Too much wood for my taste.'

He spoke to the woman behind the bar. She put down two glasses in front of Sam and Andrew and filled each about a quarter full with some white wine. Andrew sipped his and found it pleasant. But before he had even finished it Sam had ordered another wine for them to taste. Andrew gathered that the tasting was free, but that it was considered proper, after enough sampling, to buy two or three bottles to take away. He was not sure how much he had drunk by the time Sam decided that they had sampled enough and bought three bottles of the first wine that they had tried.

But that was not the end of their wine-tasting on the journey. They were in the wine country of South Australia now and soon after they had driven off they reached another winery where Sam again turned in to buy another two or three bottles for Denis. He and Andrew again went through the ritual of tasting, bought some bottles and drove on. By the time that they had visited four wineries and accumulated a very generous present for Denis, Andrew began to have a curious feeling that he was getting drunk. It seemed impossible, because there had been such very small quantities of wine in each of the many glasses that had been pressed upon him, but he felt a slight dizziness and an uncertainty in his legs as they walked towards the car. Seeing Sam get in behind the wheel, he hoped that his near-sighted host had a better head than he had.

It was half past five when they drove up to the door of the Gardiners' bungalow. There was a faint breeze off the sea and the air felt refreshingly cool after the heat of Hartwell. Sam went up to the door and rang the bell. Andrew heard it ring inside the house, but no one came to answer it. Sam rang again and then tried hammering on the door with the knocker, but there was still no response.

'Just a minute,' he said and went along the drive-in to the garage. He returned almost at once. 'The Holden isn't there,' he said. 'Looks as if they've been kept at Headquarters. If they have, I suppose there's no guessing how long they'll be there. Of course it was a mistake for Jan to come to me. Looks suspicious. She ought to have gone down to the rest of you on the beach and got Tony to call the police straight away. But I understand how she felt. They gave her such a bad time when Luke was killed that all she wanted was to get away.'

'Did you believe her story about how she found her sister's body, but didn't see or hear anything else?' Andrew asked.

'Asking questions again,' Sam said. 'I thought you'd decided against it.'

'Sorry, a lapse,' Andrew said. 'I won't expect an answer. But what do we do now? Sit in the car and wait?'

'No, I think we'll go over to Denis,' Sam answered. 'I feel I ought to call in on him in any case. The poor devil may be in a pretty bad way. Let's go.'

They got back into the car and drove the short distance to the Lightfoots' house.

Loaded with the bottles that Sam had bought on the drive, they went up to the door and he rang the bell. It was answered almost immediately by Denis. He might have been waiting on the other side of the door, expecting them.

'Oh, it's you!' he exclaimed when he saw Sam. 'Thank God! I thought it was the press back again. I was all ready to tell them to go to hell.'

His normally neat, oval face was strained and haggard. His eyelids were red and swollen, as if he had wept. When he showed his teeth in what the day before had seemed a pleasant if rather expressionless smile, they gave his face the grinning look of a skull. The brown hair that was receding from his forehead stood up in dishevelled strands, as if it had not been combed that day.

'I wasn't going to talk to any bloody journalist again,' he said. 'Enough is enough. Nice of you to come, Sam. D'you know where Jan is? She's vanished.'

'She's with the police,' Sam said. 'She and Tony. You needn't worry about them. Look, we brought these for you.' He gestured at the bottles that he and Andrew were carrying. 'Happened to be passing Calthorpe's and one or two other places, so we thought we might as well stock in a bit for you.'

'I see. Thanks. Nice of you to think of it.' There was a confused look in Denis's eyes and he did not seem really to take in what Sam had said. 'Come in. But where's Jan been?'

Sam stepped into the house and Andrew followed him.

'She came to me,' Sam said, 'and the police came after her. But she doesn't know anything. She didn't see anything. She came out of the bedroom where she'd been changing and found Kay dead and panicked and drove straight up to Hartwell. Silliest thing she could have done, with the police still trying to pin Luke's murder on her, or so she believes. I'm not sure if she's right about that and I'm sick and tired of hearing about it by now. Sometimes I wish I'd murdered the bastard myself, it would have saved a lot of trouble. I often felt like doing it when she told me how he was treating her. I know he'd looks and charm and money and all that, but if ever there was a brute who deserved getting murdered, it was Luke Wilding.'

'Talking of money . . .' Denis began and stopped.

Sam had put the bottles that he was carrying down on the floor of the hall and Andrew had put his load down beside them.

'Well, at least that's something you don't have to worry about,' Sam said. 'Kay's death can't make any difference to you there. No one can say you murdered her for her money.'

'No, but still it's very strange . . .' Denis began again and once more stopped. Then he went on, 'Come into the lounge. Everything's in a mess since those men were here, but we can sit down. D'you feel like a beer?'

'Sounds good to me,' Sam said. 'What about you, Andrew?'

'Thank you, yes,' Andrew answered.

Denis led the way into the living-room which the day before Andrew had thought very charming. It was in disorder now, with the powder that the fingerprint men had used leaving a grey film on all the polished surfaces and the hearthrug that had been stained with Kay's blood and the crystal that had killed her removed. It was desolate, and in spite of the warmth of the evening seemed to have a chill in it. Denis left them for a few minutes, returning with glasses of beer on a tray. As he handed one to Andrew he seemed for the first time to become aware of his presence.

'This isn't what you came to Australia for,' he said with a strained attempt at a smile. 'I suppose you'll be making for home soon instead of staying on.'

'I haven't thought about it yet,' Andrew answered and realized with some surprise that this was true. He had wondered if he was more of a burden or a help to Tony and whether or not it might be best for him to move to a hotel, but it had not occurred to him to return to England yet. He began to wonder now if it was really what he ought to do.

'You were saying something about money, Denis,' Sam said. He had sat down in an armchair, stretching out his thin, hairy legs with one ankle crossed over the other. 'What's the problem?'

'It's only that Vaughan, our lawyer, was out here today,' Denis said, standing where the hearthrug had been and leaning an elbow on the mantelpiece. 'I thought it was best to get in touch with him and tell him what had happened and he came out here and told me—not that it's important, but it's odd—he told me he doesn't know anything about what Kay did with her money, or where it came from. And nor do the people at our bank. He's got her will. We both made wills after we got married and left everything we had to one another, and that's quite straightforward, but he hasn't any share certificates or records of where her money came from or where she kept it. That doesn't seem important now, but I suppose we'll have to get it sorted out sooner or later for probate. It's just an additional little worry.'

'I don't understand,' Sam said. 'She hadn't any money. Not that I knew of.'

'She had,' Denis said. 'I don't know how much, but she certainly had money of her own. Investments, I always supposed, she'd inherited from her mother. I never questioned her about them, because I knew she liked to handle them herself, but she had enough to buy her own clothes and keep us in luxuries I couldn't have afforded on my salary.'

'Her poor mother hadn't a cent,' Sam said.

'Could she have inherited it from someone else, then?' Denis asked. 'Some aunt or uncle.'

Sam shook his head. 'We never went in for money in my family.'

'It doesn't matter now, anyway,' Denis said. 'We'll get it sorted out in time.'

'Could she have been earning it on the quiet?' Andrew asked. 'I once knew a woman who was married to the Governor of some African country and she found she could make a very nice income writing romantic stories, well spiced with sex, for magazines at home. But she didn't think they were what most people out there in those days would have thought the Governor's lady ought to be writing, so she gave herself a pseudonym, opened an account under that name in one of the banks there, and contributed handsomely to the family budget without her husband knowing anything about it. Could Kay have been doing anything like that?'

'Kay never wrote a line in her life,' Sam said.

'I really don't think she did,' Denis said. 'But perhaps you've hit on it, Andrew. I mean, that she was earning money somehow which for some reason she liked to keep secret.'

As he spoke the sound of the front doorbell pealed through the house. Quietly, under his breath, Denis began to swear. Then the bell pealed again.

'It'll be that man, Ross,' Denis muttered. 'He said he'd

be back again sometime. Let him go on ringing. I haven't got to let him in.'

'I think I would, if I were you,' Sam said. 'No point in antagonizing these people. Shall I open the door for you?'

Denis gave a deep sigh. 'No, I'll go.'

He got up to go to the front door. Seeing him from the back, Andrew realized how weary the man was, how his shoulders had slumped, his spine sagged, and how his feet dragged on the ground, so that he looked twenty years older than he was. Andrew heard him open the front door, then give a startled exclamation.

'What are *you* doing here?' he asked.

'Can I come in?' the very English voice of the Honourable Dudley Blair said. 'There's something I've got to tell you.'

'Have you got to do it now?' Denis asked. 'I've had about all I can take. If you could do it some other time, Dud—'

'No, no, at once, the sooner the better.' The young man's voice sounded excited, almost frenzied, as if he were ready to make trouble if he were resisted. 'I promise I'll keep it short. It won't take long. But I've got to tell you about it.'

'All right, then, come in.'

Andrew heard the door close, then saw Dudley Blair appear in the doorway of the living-room. He was in his usual rags, his feet were bare and his toenails were painted. There was a curious animation in his eyes and his cheeks were flushed.

'You see, it's all my fault,' he said in a loud, aggressive voice. 'I've got to confess to someone.'

He collided with the doorpost as he said it, then subsided gently, all six foot three of him, on to the floor.

CHAPTER 6

'He's drunk,' Sam said.

'I'm not sure he is.' Andrew got up and stooped over the young man. He remembered a student who had once come aggressively into his room to argue with him about something, then had quietly collapsed, just as Dudley Blair had done. 'I think it may be something else.'

'Then hadn't we better get a doctor?' Denis said.

'If I'm right, it might be better not to,' Andrew said. 'It might only make trouble for him. I don't think he's actually unconscious, you know.'

'What do you think is the matter with him?' Sam asked.

'Pot,' Andrew said. 'Hashish. Cannabis. Whatever you like to call it. A slight overdose.'

His guess was based partly on what Jan and Tony had told him about Dudley.

'What ought we to do about it?' Denis asked. 'We can't leave him just lying there.'

'I believe strong coffee is as good as anything,' Andrew said.

'I'll make some,' Denis said and disappeared to the kitchen.

'Let's get him up on to the settee,' Sam said.

Between them he and Andrew lifted the young man, whose long, thin body was very light. They put him down on the sofa and put a cushion under his head. He groaned as they were doing it, opened his eyes and muttered something like a protest, then closed them again and lay limply where they had put him.

'These kids,' Sam said. 'What fools they are. I wonder where he gets it. Do you think he meant what he said?'

'That he wanted to confess to the murder?'

'That's what it sounded like, didn't it?'

'I don't think it would be surprising if he's had second thoughts about that by the time he comes round,' Andrew said. 'On the other hand, it may have been something else he wanted to confess, which he may tell us about presently.'

'Jan's fond of him,' Sam said. 'She's told me about him. She's sorry for him and she's kept trying to help him. My own idea is it's time someone told him to get down to a plain job of work.'

Andrew did not think that the matter was as simple as that. He had met other Dudley Blairs during his working life, had been sorry for them, irritated by them and defeated by them, and he had never come even close to making up his mind what ought to be done with them.

By the time that Denis returned with the coffee, Dudley was certainly conscious. He had shifted his position on the sofa, drawing his long legs up so that his feet did not protrude beyond the end of it and giving a sudden violent shiver as if the shock of returning to the normal world were almost too painful to be borne. His eyes were still closed, but when the coffee was brought he opened them again and observed in his well-bred voice, 'This is terribly good of you.'

'Better sit up,' Sam said and put his hands out to haul the young man into a sitting posture, but he attained that himself without help. Denis poured out a cup of coffee and brought it to him and seemed prepared to hold it to his lips, but Dudley took the cup from him and held it only a little shakily to his lips.

'Good,' he said. 'Very good. I'm so sorry this happened. Not what I intended at all. I never dreamt it would. I didn't mean to be any trouble to anyone.'

All the aggressiveness was gone.

'Has it never happened to you before?' Andrew asked.

'Well, yes, once or twice. But of course one's never expecting it when it comes. It always takes one by surprise. Everything seems so wonderfully clear and simple beforehand. And I knew it was important to come and see Denis, but it would have been better if I'd put it off for a time, wouldn't it?'

'Why did you come to see me?' Denis asked.

Dudley's forehead wrinkled in a puzzled frown. 'Yes, why did I? I expect I'll remember in a moment. This coffee is very good.'

'Have some more.' Denis refilled his cup.

'Thank you,' Dudley said. 'It's terribly good of you. But I'm really sorry to be so much trouble.'

'Never mind about that.' Denis had drawn a chair up beside the sofa and sat down close to it, his gaze fixed intently on Dudley's face. 'You said you'd got to confess to someone. You also said it was your fault. What were you talking about? Kay's death?'

'Well, I was and I wasn't. I didn't kill her, if that's what you want to know. I'm pretty sure I didn't. It's all a bit hazy at the moment, but no, I'm sure I didn't. But I feel I'm to blame for it.'

'For God's sake, what are you talking about?' Denis asked impatiently. 'Can't you say what you mean?'

'I don't think it's much good trying to hurry him,' Andrew said. 'He'll tell you all about it soon.'

'Yes, of course,' Dudley said, 'only it's confusing. There are so many things to tell. I've spent most of the day with the police—that's one thing I want to tell you about. Then there's the business of the tall man I saw when I was jogging —that's another. And then there's the thing I specially wanted to tell you . . .' He frowned again with the effort of concentration. 'You see, I told Jan where I'd been getting my pot. I shouldn't have done that, but d'you know, it didn't occur to me she didn't know all about it. I mean, working in the place herself, you'd have thought she'd have been bound to know. But she didn't. It was a great shock to her. And she said she'd have to think over what she ought to do. And what she did was talk it over with Kay and that's how all the trouble started.'

'Just a minute,' Denis said. 'You say you've been getting your drugs from the shop where Jan works.'

'That's it.'

'In other words, you've been getting them from Sara Massingham.'

Dudley gave a reluctant nod of his head. 'Yes.'

114

'How did you pay her?' Denis asked. 'Isn't it an expensive hobby?'

'I didn't pay her,' Dudley said. 'I'd just take along some of my stuff from time to time—my jewellery, you know—and she wouldn't pay me, she'd just hand over a few joints, not many, because my stuff isn't really worth much, but she liked it and generally managed to sell it quite profitably. And of course I thought Jan knew all about it, but the poor girl was really upset. I tried to tell her it was nothing so very dreadful, not like heroin or cocaine, but she wouldn't listen, and I was afraid she was going to go straight to the police with what I'd told her, but instead she told me next day she'd talked it over with Kay and Kay had told her to leave the matter with her.'

'She always talked everything over with Kay,' Sam said. 'That at least sounds true.'

'It's all true, everything I've said,' Dudley asserted.

'Where's Sara been getting the stuff from?' Denis asked. 'Do you know that?'

'Her brother's skipper of a ship that trades in Indonesia,' Dudley answered. 'I think he's been bringing it in.'

'How much of this have you told the police?'

Dudley gave a deep sigh. 'All of it. They came and picked me up because someone had told them I'd been given a green towel by Jan, and they'd found one just like it with bloodstains on the beach. I don't know how they found out about my having one, but they knew all about it. It rather puzzled me.'

'I told them,' Andrew said. 'If you remember, I was there when you came to the Gardiners' house and picked it up.'

'Yes—yes, I remember now. I hadn't thought of that. Actually I was able to show them that I still had the towel and that it hadn't any bloodstains on it. But I've been in trouble with them before, you see, about pot. Nothing serious. They picked several of us up at a party and lectured us and let us go. But this time they'd got it into their heads

Kay's death might somehow be connected with the drugs racket and kept on at me till I told them everything I knew.'

'And you think yourself Kay's death may really have been connected with it?' Andrew said.

Dudley squirmed slightly from embarrassment on the sofa.

'It does look like it, doesn't it?' he said.

'But what did she do to make herself immediately so dangerous to someone that she had to be killed?'

'I don't like to tell you what I think.'

'Go on,' Denis said savagely. 'You've said enough already. Tell us the rest of it.'

'It's just that it seemed to me possible that she'd threatened Sara somehow,' Dudley said, 'and Sara had told her brother, or whoever else she was working with, and they did the job.'

'My God, you're saying Kay tried to blackmail Sara!' Denis's voice had dropped almost to a whisper, yet it sounded far more dangerous than his explosion of the moment before. He looked as if he were having trouble keeping his hands to himself instead of fastening them round the thin neck of the young man. 'Isn't that what you're leading up to?'

Dudley turned his head on the cushion so that he did not have to meet Denis's eyes. 'It might not have been blackmail, you know,' he said. 'She may simply have threatened to go to the police. Isn't that much more likely?'

Andrew was not sure that it was. From the time that Denis had spoken of Kay's mysterious income he had wondered uneasily, in spite of the feeling that the explanation was too melodramatic, if blackmail might not have been the source of it. The thought would probably never have occurred to him if Sam had not told him that she was greedy, ambitious and unscrupulous. Indeed, it would have seemed fantastic. Until murder had invaded the scene here there had been an air of quietly smart respectability about the Lightfoots and their home that would have made such a thing seem preposterous. But mysterious incomes, apparently paid in this instance in cash, since neither her husband, her lawyer, nor her bank had any record of it, have to come from somewhere, which made blackmail a possibility that perhaps ought to be considered.

But there was something about this that did not fit. It was only a few days since Kay had heard of Sara Massingham's connection with the distribution of drugs, yet as he understood what Denis had said about it, Kay had had an income of her own at least since the time that they were married.

'Are you sure,' Andrew asked, 'that Kay didn't know that Miss Massingham was handling drugs before you said anything about it to Jan?'

'One can't be *sure* about a thing like that, can one?' Dudley answered.

'I can be bloody sure she didn't know,' Denis said, suddenly directing his anger at Andrew. 'For one thing, can you believe that if Kay had been blackmailing Sara, she would have come to dinner with us, or that Kay would have asked her? And you're forgetting I know Kay rather well. She wasn't a blackmailer, she wasn't a drug peddler, and even if she'd heard about the drugs from Jan and decided to go to the police about it, she wouldn't have done that without talking it over with me. We loved each other, you know. And we had a way of talking most things over together if we had problems. And it's bad enough that she's dead without having foul insinuations made about her.'

There was an over-emphasis in his voice which had the effect of making him sound less sure of what he was saying than he intended.

Sam drew attention to his presence with a cough. 'Just what I was thinking myself,' he said. 'But you, Dudley, you said something about a tall man you saw when you were jogging. What was that all about?'

Dudley thrust a hand through his yellow curls, pushing

them back from his forehead on which small beads of sweat were visible. He looked as if he were turning sulky.

'I don't suppose there's anything in that,' he muttered.

'But what was it you saw?' Sam asked.

'Just a man who came down the steps from the road to the beach. Could have been anybody.'

'But why did you notice him? What did he look like?'

'I couldn't see, because he'd got a towel draped over his head and shoulders. And that's why I noticed him. The towel had the same pattern on it as the one Jan lent me. But I didn't stop to take a look at him. No reason why I should. I was out jogging along the beach and I'd got past him before he'd got anywhere near the water.'

'But you saw him come down the steps?'

'Yes.'

'So he could have been coming from here.'

'That's what I thought at the time. I knew the Lightfoots were having some sort of party, so I thought it was probably Tony. But that doesn't seem likely now. I mean, with those bloodstains on it and all.'

'Isn't there anything you can tell us about him?' Sam asked. 'You said he was tall.'

'Yes.'

'How tall?'

'Oh, just tall. Tallish. Not as tall as me.'

'Say six foot?'

Dudley nodded. 'Just about.'

Sam turned to Andrew with a sardonic smile. 'You're just about six foot, I'd say, Andrew, and you'd access to Jan's towels. Feel like confessing?'

Andrew shook his head. 'No, I'm not in the mood for it just now, Sam. But it's a fact that there were several tall men here yesterday. Denis, Tony and Bob are all about six foot. Nicholl isn't as tall as they are, but he's well-built and if one were simply jogging past and he was on the steps above one, I think one might think he was fairly tall. But I wonder if you could be persuaded to confess yourself, Sam.'

A little to his surprise, because he had intended his tone to match Sam's in slightly macabre flippancy, Andrew saw an uneasy glint appear in Sam's grey eyes.

'I guess I'm not in the mood for it either,' he muttered.

'I believe there's one thing you could tell us, if only you would,' Andrew said.

'What's that?'

'The real reason Jan ran away to you.'

Andrew saw a stubborn look appear on Sam's face and he knew that he would not get an answer to his question, or if he did, that it was unlikely to be true. Not that Sam might not believe it himself, or at most feel only faintly suspicious that Jan had lied to him. But either she or Sam or both of them had lied, Andrew felt fairly sure of it by now.

'She told you, didn't she?' Sam said.

'That she'd lost her head? That she was so scared she only wanted to get away?' Andrew gave his head a slight shake. 'I dare say it's my own fault, some blind patch I've got, but I find it awfully difficult to believe that that's the whole of the story.'

The glint in Sam's eyes brightened with anger. Andrew began to regret what he had said. He realized that he was probably going to have a quarrel with Sam and he did not want one. It was not only that he liked the man, but to let the mood in the room become destructively emotional would be less than useful. He thought of the violence that had happened there the day before and felt sickened by the sense of it that he suddenly felt in the group of them there.

'You can believe anything you bloody well want to believe,' Sam said harshly. 'It's nothing to me.'

Denis, who had become very pale, said, 'What are you trying to say, Andrew?'

'I don't know,' Andrew admitted. 'I believe she was scared and was running away from something, but I'm not sure what. I think she may have seen the murderer.'

'And wouldn't that have scared you?' Sam said, his voice rising. 'I thought you'd decided against asking questions. Go on with this sort of thing and you'll get egg on your face.'

'Quite right,' Andrew said. 'I won't go on.'

'Why not?' Denis asked. His voice was very quiet compared with Sam's, but had a dangerous ring in it. 'If you've some idea in your head about what made her do what she did, it's up to you to tell us what it is. So go on!'

'It's nothing as definite as an idea,' Andrew said. 'It's just a feeling that she may have seen the murderer and for some reason was afraid to go down to us on the beach and tell us what she'd seen.'

'Afraid of what he might do to her if she did?' Denis asked.

'Something like that.'

'But if she'd run away from him and come down to us straight away and told us what had happened, what could he have done to her?'

'That's the question. But suppose he'd some way of preventing her talking. Suppose, for instance, he'd some sort of hold over her so that she couldn't talk, and yet she couldn't face going down to us and behaving in front of us as if nothing had happened. That might have been a very good reason for running away. At least it would have given her time to calm down. Didn't she give you a hint of anything like that, Sam?'

'She did not. She told me just what she told you and Tony and that's enough for me. A hold over her! Who the hell could have a hold over her, a kid who'd never done anyone any harm? You've got to harm someone or do something crooked before you give them a hold over you. I'm not staying here to listen to any more of this. I'm going along to see if Jan and Tony have got home yet. You can come along and join me there later if you want to, Andrew.'

Without waiting to hear what Andrew wanted to do, he turned to the door and slouched out of the room.

He left silence behind him until after a little Denis observed, 'You frightened him, Andrew.'

'I rather think I did,' Andrew said. 'I didn't mean to. I was just thinking the thing out as I talked. But perhaps I got closer to the truth than I realized.'

Denis had got up from the chair beside the sofa where Dudley Blair still lay and began to walk about the room.

'Of course there's something you didn't say,' he said after a moment. 'I wonder if it's possible . . .' He stared broodingly at the floor before him.

Dudley spoke up brightly. 'Professor Basnett didn't say that Jan may actually have wanted to protect the murderer.'

'Shut up!' Denis snarled. 'Let me think. Yes, it's possible. It's possible, you see, that it was Sam himself who did the murder.'

'Oh come,' Andrew said. 'His own daughter?'

'What's wrong with that? The majority of murders are done by people who are very close to the victim: the husband, the wife, the father, the son. It's within a family that the worst hatred is usually generated. And Sam never cared for Kay. We all knew that. He didn't try to conceal it. And he's got a violent temper. He was like Luke in that. Perhaps that's what drew Jan to Luke, the good old father fixation. You haven't seen it, Andrew, but I've seen Sam purple in the face and shaking all over with rage over a mere nothing. It's the kind of temper that comes out of nowhere and disappears as suddenly as it comes and in a moment he'll have forgotten it ever happened. Because it disappears so quickly people have a way of forgiving it, yet while it's got hold of him I swear he'd be capable of anything.'

'Even murder?'

'Even murder.'

'Without a motive?'

'Oh, he'd have had a motive of sorts. Just for the moment. Suppose it happened like this. Suppose he came down from Hartwell by plane. When he comes to visit us, which isn't a thing he does very often, he generally comes by plane because he's got poor eyesight and doesn't care for driving so far. So suppose he came down by plane because he suddenly got it into his head it would be nice to visit us on Christmas Day, then got to Adelaide, took a taxi from the airport and walked in on Kay while Jan was in the bedroom, changing. He may have been full of the Christmas spirit, goodwill and alcohol combined, and instead of welcoming him Kay may have said something, done something . . . To tell the truth, she wasn't the most tactful of people. But it could have been something as trivial as telling him he'd been drinking too much on the plane, or perhaps not saying thank you with enough enthusiasm for some present he'd brought her. And he lost that foul temper of his, picked up that damned lump of crystal and banged her on the head.'

'Just a minute,' Andrew said. 'Do planes go on Christmas Day?'

'Oh yes,' Denis answered. 'Cheapest day of the whole year to travel. Sam wouldn't have been thinking of murder and probably didn't mean to hit as hard as he did, but he's very strong and for the moment he'd have been blind to what he was doing. And then Jan came in and found him with the crystal in his hand and Kay dead at his feet and him just beginning to come to his senses. So it's obvious what she did then, isn't it?'

'If any of this is true, yes,' Andrew said. 'I suppose he'd be in a pretty dazed condition at what he'd done and she'd just have led him home, packed him into the Volvo and driven off to Hartwell. It certainly acounts for her behaviour. But there's one thing that doesn't fit in.'

'The towel!' Dudley Blair cried. 'How did that blood-stained towel get down to the beach?'

'Shut up!' Denis snarled at him again. 'You've done enough damage already.'

'But it's just what I was going to say,' Andrew said.

Denis thought it over, then gave a brief nod, as if he had arrived at a conclusion that was convincing, at least to himself.

'Of course it was Jan who took it down before going home,' he said, 'just to create confusion.'

'But it was a man I saw, a tall man,' Dudley protested. 'I swear it was.'

'You were jogging past,' Denis said. 'I've watched joggers and they seem to be quite unaware of anything that's going on around them. They're completely wrapped up in themselves. You just think that you saw a tall man. Perhaps you didn't even really think it. It may be something you thought up when the police started putting pressure on you because you're fond of Jan and didn't want to cast suspicion on her!'

'It was a tall man,' Dudley said stubbornly. 'I'll swear to that in court.'

'Then there's only one other possibility,' Denis said. 'Tony came into the house, I suppose to find out why Kay and Jan hadn't come down to join us, found out what had happened, and to help Jan and Sam, took the towel down to the beach, as I said, to confuse things. It was Tony who pointed out the towel to us there, wasn't it, and who brought it in to show to the police? He could have been making sure it didn't get overlooked.'

'On the other hand . . .' Andrew said and paused.

'Yes?' Denis said.

'I don't really believe in this theory of yours at all. I don't think Sam was here yesterday. I think when the police start making inquiries in Hartwell, as I'm sure they will, because naturally they'll have thought of this possibility for themselves, they'll find someone who saw him there and can give him an alibi.'

'Perhaps,' Denis said. 'Perhaps. I'll tell you something

else, though. I can't say I've evidence for it, it's just something I've always felt. I believe Sam knows a lot more about Luke Wilding's murder than he's ever admitted.'

'That would mean Jan knows more about it than she's ever admitted,' Andrew said.

'Suppose she does?'

'Then I grant you she may have told Sam about it. But I thought it was generally accepted that she couldn't have done the murder herself, because she couldn't have moved the body down to the pool.'

'She could have had an accomplice.'

'Who, for instance? Her father himself, or Tony? And even if she had one, it still doesn't explain the reason why the body was moved.'

'There's a theory it was done to get it to a car and drive it off into the bush and bury it,' Denis said, 'but that someone else appeared on the scene and the murderer, or the accomplice, or whoever it was, had to drop the body in a hurry and bolt.'

'I've heard that theory,' Andrew said, 'but I don't much like it, though I admit I can't think of a better one.'

As he said it, however, Andrew felt that he had missed the point of something. Something had been said in the last few minutes the point of which he had failed to understand. Perhaps he had even said it himself. This was not altogether an unusual experience for him. His mind had never moved swiftly, which had always been a disadvantage to him in his work. He was slow at making points in an argument. It might be hours after the argument had closed that he would think of the retort that he ought so obviously to have made. On committees he had usually been one of the silent members, because he would generally find himself trying to disentangle what had seemed wrong to him about something that had been said five minutes before when a new controversy was already raging round him. The feeling came to him now that if only he could force his mind to hurry up a little, he might be able to add something significant to what Denis had been saying.

But besides his normal slowness, he was suffering acutely from fatigue. He thought that it might really be best if he took his leave of Denis and followed Sam to the Gardiners' bungalow, hoping that there would be someone there by now to let him in. If there was, he thought, he would go straight to bed. He was not in the least hungry. He could do without a meal, but he yearned, as he had after the flight from Heathrow, to get out of the clothes that he had been wearing for far too long, and fall asleep.

Getting up, he began to say, 'I think I'll be off, Denis,' when the front doorbell rang again.

This time it was Tony. He was looking very tired also, though with an air of nervous tension about him which suggested that even if he went to bed, he had not much hope of sleep. Denis offered him beer and he accepted it absently and seemed to feel no need for a moment to explain what had brought him, but sinking down into a chair, sipped a little beer and closed his eyes.

When he opened them again, they settled on Dudley and looked startled, as if he had only just become aware of the fact that the young man was there.

'What are you doing here, Dud?' he asked.

'Let's not go into that now,' Denis said. 'I'll tell you about that later. You look just about finished, Tony. What have they been doing to you?'

'The police?' Tony said. 'Questions, questions, questions. Then tea and sandwiches, then more questions.'

'Where's Jan?' Denis asked.

'At home. Feeling crook. Gone to bed. Dad came in soon after we got there and told us you were here, Andrew, so I thought I'd better come along and collect you.'

'I was just coming,' Andrew said.

'I'm sorry we've got you into all this,' Tony said.

'Not exactly your fault.'

'Well, I don't know. I needn't have taken you up to Hartwell. If it comes to that, I needn't have gone myself. Shouldn't have gone, in fact. Sam was right: When we drove off the police followed us and caught up with Jan before she'd time to get hold of herself. She's in a real mess now, contradicting herself every time she opens her mouth. It was just that I was so bloody scared the murderer had got her. But I've never seen her cry so much as she has today, and that damned man Ross kept offering her tea. More and more tea. She wasn't much use to him when she was crying. It was mostly for Kay, of course. They were very fond of one another. But also it was from shock and fear. I can't help feeling she knows more than she'll tell even me, though she may have told it to Dad. She keeps talking about Luke, almost as if he was alive, and once she called Dad Luke by mistake and didn't even realize she'd done it.'

'Perhaps you should call a doctor,' Denis said.

'I thought I'd see how she is tomorrow,' Tony answered.

'He could give her a sedative tonight. But I expect you're right to wait, though you look as if you could do with a sedative yourself.'

Tony finished his drink at a gulp. 'I'm all right.' He stood up. 'Coming, Andrew?'

The front doorbell rang yet again. Reluctantly Denis went out into the hall.

When he opened the door, a shouting voice greeted him, a harsh, wildly excited voice.

'Have you heard what they've done?' it shouted. 'You won't believe it. They've arrested Sara. Sara! Has everyone gone mad?'

His blue eyes blazing and his handsome, hollow-cheeked face feverishly patched with red, Bob Wilding burst into the room.

'For trafficking in drugs . . .' he was beginning when his gaze fell on Dudley Blair, who had stood up and was facing him across the room.

Bob Wilding stood still, rigid, just inside the doorway. A look almost of disbelief appeared on his face.

'So you're here,' he said incredulously, his voice dropping almost to a whisper. 'The one place I didn't think of. I've been hunting for you everywhere.'

'I'm sorry,' Dudley said. 'I suppose you're the person I ought to have got in touch with when the police let me go.'

'Oh, you suppose that, do you?' Bob Wilding said, his voice furiously sarcastic and his rigidity changing to a suppressed kind of trembling.

In another moment, Andrew thought, he was going to launch himself across the room at Dudley. Recognizing with dismay that even if he tried to prevent what seemed likely to happen, it was unlikely that a man of his age would be able to do anything useful, he was glad to see that Tony took a step forward.

But Dudley did not seem disturbed.

'I'm really sorry,' he said. 'The fact is, there was something I wanted to tell Denis. I thought I owed it to him to tell it straight away, because I believe that in a way I'm to blame for what happened here. You see, I told Jan—' He stopped abruptly, looking doubtfully at the enraged man facing him.

'What did you tell Jan?' Bob demanded. 'That Sara had been peddling drugs to you?'

'Well, yes,' Dudley said.

'You lying bastard!' Bob shouted, his voice shaking. 'She's never done anything but try to help you.'

'Yes, I know that,' Dudley said pacifically. 'She was only trying to help me when she slipped me a few cigarettes from time to time. She knew I needed them and I was very grateful. They really were a great help when things went badly wrong with me, as they sometimes do. I get these terrible fits of depression, you see. You just don't know what they're like. They're why I couldn't stay at home and thought I'd come to Australia. I thought it would be different here, but of course it hasn't been. The trouble was nothing to do with my home and family, as I used to think, it's something in me and I take it with me wherever I go. But I oughtn't to have talked about the thing to Jan—the pot, I mean. Only I took for granted she must know about it if she worked in the shop—'

With a strangled sort of roar, Bob dived across the room at Dudley. Bob's hands were raised, as if he were reaching for the other's throat. Dudley stood still with a look of puzzled distress on his face. What he might have done in the way of defending himself if Bob had reached him Andrew did not discover, because before he could do so Tony had lunged forward and grasped one of Bob's arms and Denis had made a grab at the other. While they did so, Andrew placed himself between Bob and Dudley, though he did not think he would really be much use there if Bob freed himself from the other two men, but at least it felt better than doing nothing.

'Take it easy, Bob,' Tony said. 'All right, there's been a mistake of some sort somewhere, but this sort of thing isn't going to help.'

'Too right, it won't!' Bob shouted. 'You just let me go and I'll teach him a thing or two!'

'But I said I was sorry,' Dudley said, sounding like a small boy who was about to be punished for having broken something unintentionally.

'Come and sit down, Bob,' Denis said, 'and listen to the rest of the story. Then perhaps we can sort out what really happened.'

Unwillingly Bob allowed himself to be thrust into a chair. Both Tony and Denis remained standing on either side of him in case he should take it into his head to make another attack on Dudley.

'Go on, Dud,' Tony said, 'Denis may have heard this, but I haven't.'

'It's just that I mentioned the pot to Jan,' Dudley said,

128

'and instead of knowing all about it, as I thought she would, it turned out to be pretty much of a shock to her, and she talked it over with Kay and Kay told her to leave the matter to her. And then, you see, Kay was murdered.'

Denis spoke bitterly. 'You've left out the bit this time about Kay probably having blackmailed Sara.'

'Has he said that?' Bob demanded fiercely. 'And hasn't he said Sara murdered Kay?'

'Actually he hasn't,' Andrew said. He had moved away to a chair and sat down. It was disturbing to realize that the brief spell of violence in the room had made his heart beat surprisingly uncomfortably. For the first time he wondered if there was anything the matter with his heart. He had always taken for granted that it was one of the soundest parts of him. But every trouble has to have a beginning, and this might be the start of something. 'He suggested that Kay threatened Miss Massingham,' he went on, 'or perhaps warned would be a better word, that she was going to tell the police about the matter, and Miss Massingham told her brother, or whoever it was from whom she was getting the drugs, and it was he who murdered Kay.'

'That's just as bad,' Bob said. 'It would make Sara part of a conspiracy. And it's all so infamous, a lie from start to finish. Can't you see why he's made it up?'

'I suppose to conceal the source from which he's really been getting the drugs,' Andrew said, 'if it wasn't Miss Massingham.'

'You can bet that's it!' Bob said. 'And I'll soon get that out of him if you'll let me get at him.'

'You know, Dudley,' Andrew said, 'I think you might be wise to leave.'

'But I can't while he still thinks I'm lying,' Dudley said plaintively. 'Really I'm not, Bob. I dare say I've misunderstood something and got a bit mixed up, but it's absolutely true I've been getting an occasional joint from Sara, and I told Jan about it, and Jan told me she'd talk it over with

129

Kay and then told me Kay said she should leave the matter to her. All those things are *facts*. Anything else is speculation, but those things are facts and they're absolutely all I've told the police.'

'So you've told all this rubbish to the police, have you?' Bob said with the tremor of rage back in his voice. 'I might have known it.'

'I couldn't help it,' Dudley said apologetically. 'I couldn't help feeling that with something so serious under discussion, I'd got to tell them the truth. But it's a funny thing, they didn't seem much interested. It was my impression that they knew about it already. I mean, about Sara. I think they've been watching her for some time, trying to find out who's been supplying her. Assuming it's her brother who's been getting the stuff on his trips to Indonesia, I suppose they've been watching to catch him with a consignment.'

'I wonder if her brother's in the country now,' Tony said, 'and if he is, I wonder if he's got an alibi for yesterday afternoon.'

'And I wonder if he's a tall man,' Andrew said. 'Have you ever seen him, Bob?'

Bob lifted his clenched fists and beat his temples with them.

'I don't believe it! I don't believe any of it! It's all a childish lie!' he screamed.

'But have you seen him?' Tony asked.

'No!'

'Well, I think Andrew and I may as well go home,' Tony said. 'But you go first, Dud.'

'It's all right, I won't touch him,' Bob muttered. 'Anyway, not so long as he keeps his mouth shut. If he starts talking again, I don't promise . . .'

He was still mumbling what he might do in that event when Dudley quietly left the room. A moment later Tony and Andrew followed him.

CHAPTER 7

'If you don't mind, Tony,' Andrew said as they reached the gate, 'I'd rather like to go for a short walk. Just a little way along the beach. I'll follow you presently.'

'Want some peace and quiet?' Tony said. 'Right. Will you manage to find your way back to us?'

'Oh, I think so.'

'See you later, then.' Tony set off along the road towards his home.

Andrew walked to the steps that led down to the beach, but then, instead of going down them on to the strip of sandy shore which was at its narrowest at that moment, because the tide was high, he stayed on the road above it, strolling along slowly, feeling an almost sensual pleasure in the simple absence of voices round him, in the silence that was broken only by the gentle wash of the waves over the sand.

At intervals along the side of the road there were benches, one or two of them occupied by a couple or a solitary figure, but most of them empty. The long row of Norfolk Island pines, in their dark uniforms, were like guards keeping watch on the coast, protecting the peace of the evening. The blue of the sky, which had been so brilliant earlier, had been softened by the first tinge of dusk. There was a faint opalescent sheen on the calm sea. There were no crowds, not even any cricketing children.

After he had walked only a little way, Andrew sat down on one of the benches. Resting his elbow on the back of it, he propped his head on his hand. His mind felt blessedly blank. It was wonderfully restful. The pressure of other people's emotions, their problems, their loves and hates and fears, had faded and left him in peace. It was a peace, he knew, which was not likely to last long, for he was not a callous man and this escape from their troubles could only be brief. But to have an empty mind for the moment was more comforting than he could remember such a condition ever having been before. He wondered dreamily how long he could decently stay here before returning to the Gardiners' house.

On the beach in front of him a flock of gulls had settled. They were all gazing in the same direction out to sea and were almost motionless. He believed they were called silver gulls. They were smallish, with white heads and bodies, silver grey wings and black tails. They had the stolid, rather self-satisfied air which made Andrew think of a group of business executives gathered together for a conference. One bird that had separated itself a little from the others and was standing in front of the pack, might have been their chairman. Further along the beach there was another compact group of the same kind of gull, also gazing out to sea and also motionless, but plainly wishing to have no truck with the group that was nearest to him. Then all of a sudden the further group, as if at a signal that the meeting was over, rose at the same time and flew away. Mysterious things, birds, he thought. Almost as mysterious, almost as totally beyond the understanding of a rational mind, as human beings.

Andrew's head, resting on his hand, felt very heavy. If the wooden bench had been more comfortable, he would probably have drifted off to sleep. As it was, he found himself reciting in his head, almost unconsciously:

> '"Pibroch of Donuil Dhu,
> Pibroch of Donuil,
> Wake thy wild voice anew,
> Summon Clan Conuil . . ."'

Normally it would have irritated him to find his mind possessed by the fragment of verse which in itself had no attraction for him, yet now he found that there was something soothing in it. It helped to blot out everything but the quiet of the seashore, the committee of silver gulls, the softly thumping waves, the dark, soldierly-looking pines. He repeated the lines and went on:

> '"Leave untended the herd,
> The flock without shelter,
> Leave the bride uninterred,
> The corpse at the altar . . ."'

There was something wrong with that, but he was too drowsy to think out what it was. He closed his eyes. In spite of the hardness of the bench on which he was sitting, he thought that he would soon fall asleep if he did not resist the inclination to do so. Perhaps it was time to be returning to the Gardiners' bungalow. But his head only drooped farther on to his chest . . .

'Professor Basnett.'

He started and, considering how close he had been to sleep, woke up reasonably quickly. Clare and David Nicholl were standing before him. He began to get to his feet, but Clare said quickly, 'Please don't let us disturb you. We just came out for a short walk. We often do that in the evening. The crowds have all gone and it's so quiet and nice. Then we saw you and didn't realize you were asleep.'

She sat down beside him. David remained standing.

'I wasn't alseep,' Andrew said. 'Just a bit drowsy. Tired. Very tired. It's been an exhausting day.'

'D'you know if they've found out anything about the murder?' Clare asked.

'Which murder . . . Oh, of course, you mean Kay's. I'm sorry, my mind was wandering. I don't think they have. Nothing definite. But they seem to think it's involved with drugs. I believe they've arrested Miss Massingham for trafficking in them, or at least they've taken her in for questioning, and it seems to be possible that Kay had found out something about what she was doing and that that may have been why she was killed. But I can't vouch for any of it. I was in the Lightfoots' house when Bob Wilding came in and poured it all out, but he was in a very hysterical state, practically incoherent, one might say, so it wouldn't surprise me if there's been a mistake somewhere.'

As he spoke he became more and more convinced that there had been a mistake somewhere, though he was not sure why he felt it. Something of importance, it still seemed to him, was eluding him, something that he ought to have grasped, and for some reason the presence of this young couple increased the feeling. There was something that he wanted to ask them, but what was it? They seemed to have had less to do with the events of this disastrous Christmas than anyone else whom he had met since he had come to Betty Hill.

'As a matter of fact, I'm not altogether surprised,' Clare said. 'I've always felt there was something peculiar about Sara.'

'No, you haven't,' her husband said sharply, as if he were afraid she was about to launch into indiscretions. 'You've always liked her.'

'I've always admired her,' Clare said with the self-assurance of hindsight. 'That isn't quite the same thing as liking. She's beautiful and she's clever. But I've always wondered how she kept that shop going. It isn't the kind of place out of which you can make a living. I assumed she must have some money of her own and that she ran it simply for the interest of the thing. I realized that she liked to patronize young artists like Dudley Blair. But of course, if she was dealing in drugs . . .' She gave Andrew a penetrating glance. Her unusual green eyes in her round, plump face had lost the look of certainty that they had had for a moment. She looked bewildered. 'Only you say there's been a mistake.'

'I don't know, I really don't know,' Andrew said. 'Perhaps there's no mistake about the drugs. But there's something I'd like to ask you.' His mind had begun to clear. He knew what had been eluding him. It had to do with the corpse at the altar, with the man, that was to say, who had been found dead only a few weeks after his marriage, not actually at an altar, but in a pond, where there seemed to be no good reason for him to be. 'Am I right, David, that it was you who found Luke Wilding's body? I think you told me you did.'

David Nicholl was still standing, looking as if he would have liked to move on and not have to take part in the conversation in which his wife had involved him.

'Yes, but what's that got to do with what happened yesterday?' he asked. 'Do the police think the two murders are connected?'

'I'm not in their confidence,' Andrew said, 'but I can't help feeling myself that they must be.'

'Well, I found Luke,' David said. Giving up his resistance to taking part in the discussion, he sat down beside his wife. 'But I can't tell you why his body had been dragged to the pond. I don't think anyone's been able to explain that.'

'There's a theory that the murderer was trying to drag his body to a car,' Andrew said, 'to drive it out somewhere into the bush and dump it, but then he got interrupted, perhaps by your arrival, and dropped the body and cleared out as fast as he could before you could see him.'

David nodded. 'That seems as likely to me as anything.'

'But did you see a car?'

David wrinkled his brow. 'A car? Where?'

'That's what I'd like to know,' Andrew said. 'I've never been to the quarry, so I don't know what sort of approaches to it there are, but when you got there yourself, did you see a car parked anywhere?'

'Yes, I saw Luke's car.'

'You knew it? You're sure it was his?'

'Yes, it was a Mercedes. Light blue. I couldn't swear to the number, but it was the only car of the kind that I'd ever seen in the neighbourhood. And later the police said it was his.'

'How do you get into the quarry from the road?'

'If you've a car, d'you mean, or if you're on foot?'

'Both.'

'Well, there's a sort of lay-by where I always parked if I wanted to go into the quarry. There was an old road leading in from it, but you can't really drive along it now. I don't think there was anywhere else you could have left the car if you wanted to go in. The road past the quarry is a busy main road with nowhere you can pull off it on to the verge. But of course if you were on foot you could have climbed in at a lot of places.'

'How far off is the nearest village?'

'The nearest is Hartwell. It's about ten kilometres away.'

'How far off is Wilding's sheep station?'

'From the quarry, d'you mean, or Hartwell?'

'Both,' Andrew said again.

'It's about eight or nine kilometres from the quarry, I should say,' David answered, 'and about a couple from Hartwell.'

'So if the murderer came either from Hartwell or from the sheep station on foot, and returned also on foot, he'd a good long walk before him.'

David nodded. 'That's right. I'm not sure what you're getting at, but it sounds to me as if you think he must have come by car and that could only have meant he arrived with Wilding in his Mercedes.'

'Not necessarily,' Andrew said. 'There's another possibility.'

Clare was watching him with wide-eyed concentration. 'Of course you're sure all this has something to do with Kay's murder,' she said. 'But you don't think Luke Wilding was involved in the drug traffic, do you? He'd no need of it, you know. He was a very successful grazier, with lots of money.'

'I haven't really been thinking about the drug angle,' Andrew said. 'I'm sure it's somehow connected with these murders. It would be too much of a coincidence if it weren't. But it's the car the murderer almost certainly came in that I'm interested in most.'

'And you don't think it was the Mercedes,' David said.

'I'm not sure about it. If it wasn't, it must have gone before you arrived, and that upsets the theory that you interrupted the murderer when he was dragging the body towards it. I wonder if the police found the key to the Mercedes on Wilding's body, or if it had disappeared with the murderer.'

'I can tell you that. They found it in Wilding's pocket.'

'Which may not mean much, except that you'd think if the murderer was intending to drive away in the Mercedes, he'd have made sure he could get the key and would have pocketed it himself before starting to drag Wilding all the way to the car. But of course, if he'd arrived with Wilding, he might have seen where he put the key and knew that he could get it when he got to the car.'

'But you think the murderer—he or she—didn't necessarily arrive in Wilding's car.'

'It's just that there may have been another car, as I said, that came and went earlier.'

David and Clare exchanged glances which made Andrew feel that the two of them had discussed this possibility before, even if they had never confided their doubts to anyone else. They each seemed to be trying now to discover how openly the other felt that they should talk.

They appeared to reach some wordless agreement, for David said, 'That would mean one of two things, wouldn't it? Either we're quite wrong about why the body was dumped in the billabong, or I wasn't the first person to discover it. Someone else could have arrived before me and frightened the murderer off. And that person didn't stay long, but drove away in a hurry before I got there and has never come forward to say what he saw.'

'Which may have been the murderer himself,' Clare said. 'And that would mean the murderer's been in this person's power all this time and may perhaps have been paying him blackmail. David and I have often discussed it, and we think the likeliest person—'

'No!' David interrupted swiftly. 'Don't say it. We've no evidence of any kind and we don't want to start up rumours about perfectly harmless people. Really we've no idea who it could have been, Professor.'

'Meanwhile there's that other possibility we've mentioned,' Andrew said, 'that we're wrong about why the body was dumped in the pond. Suppose the murderer wasn't interrupted by anybody. Isn't that worth thinking about?'

'But can you think of any other reason for it?' David asked.

'As a matter of fact . . .' Andrew began, but he stopped himself. Like David, he had a feeling that there might be something grievously mistaken about talking too much, even to the friendliest people, when all that he had to discuss were some shadowy suspicions. Yet the suspicions which had not even occurred to him when he started out for his stroll along the road and found the bench to rest on, were now beginning to fill his thoughts. The quiet of that short time, disturbed only by the recurrence of Donuil Dhu and the corpse that had certainly been in the wrong place, followed by his chat with the pleasant young couple, had allowed a pattern to form in his mind. A vague pattern, but one which seemed steadily to be becoming clearer.

But as it became clearer, a question became more and more insistent. What ought he to do about it?

During his working life he had never been afraid of responsibility. But the kind of responsibility that he had had to face had been fairly impersonal. It was true that he had once or twice found himself talking to a student who had decided to commit suicide and who for some reason had decided at the last moment that Andrew was the right person to tell of his intention. He had had to do his best then to dissuade the desperate child from taking such a terrible step, and once, he remembered, he had succeeded and once he had failed. When he had failed and the boy to whom he had done his very best to give some hope and reassurance had left him and straight away had swallowed a bottleful of aspirins, Andrew had felt profoundly and wretchedly inadequate. Yet the truth was that he had tended to think of such people as cases, not as friends. That made his present feeling of responsibility different.

David stood up.

'I think we'd better be going home,' he said.

'How would you like to come with us and have a bite to eat?' Clare asked. 'We live only a short way from here and there's a steak and kidney pie warming up in the oven and a peach salad. Do come.'

Andrew recognized that it gave her great pleasure to feed people, but he said, 'That's very kind of you, but I think Jan and Tony will be expecting me. They'll be wondering what's happened to me.'

Clare put a hand on his arm and gave it a little pat.

'Don't brood too much on all this,' she said as she stood up beside David. 'I know one can't stop thinking about it, but there's really nothing one can do.'

She put an arm through David's and the two of them walked away into the deepening twilight.

But Andrew did not go straight back to the Gardiners. He stayed where he was for a little, trying to arrange his thoughts. While he did so he noticed that all the gulls had flown away and that there was no one on the beach. After a while he stood up and started walking, not towards the Gardiners' house, but in the opposite direction. He knew that somewhere ahead of him was the busy suburb of

Glenelg, where it was possible, he thought, that he might find a taxi.

Reaching a wide open space which had a town hall, a police station, a hotel and a number of shops surrounding it, he stood looking about hopefully, but there were no taxis in sight. In the middle of the square, however, there was a tram.

Andrew could not remember how many years it was since he had last ridden in a tram. But there was one here on rails that ran along the centre of a street which he thought led in the direction of the city, and which had a queue of people just filing into it. Joining them, he asked if the tram did indeed go to the city and was assured that it did. Climbing aboard, he took a seat and after a brief wait found himself being jolted along in a way that rather pleasantly brought back memories of a time when travel by tram had been normal for him, while taxis had seemed unthinkably expensive.

A conductor came along the tram, collecting fares. After a look at Andrew, gauging his age, he asked him if he was a pensioner. Had he been, Andrew understood, his trip would have been free. But replying honestly that he was a foreigner and not entitled to this privilege, he paid for his ticket, then sat back, wondering whether he would really go ahead with what, while he had been sitting on the bench above the beach, had seemed to him a good idea, or whether he would simply return by the next tram and make his way to the Gardiners' house.

He had not yet entirely made up his mind about this when the tram reached its terminus, a wide square dominated by the familiar figure of Queen Victoria. It made him feel for a moment that when he had told the conductor that he was a foreigner he had not quite been speaking the truth. He was not sure how, in the modern world, he ought to describe his relationship to this far-off land, yet he did not feel altogether like a foreigner. He had felt equally foreign, if not more so, on visits to Wales, to the Hebrides, even at times to unfamiliar parts of London. He got up and made his way towards the exit.

He was about to step off the tram into the street when the conductor stopped him.

'This tram's been running since nineteen-twenty-nine,' he said with pride.

'Has it really?' Andrew said, impressed.

'That's over fifty years. There are people tried to get rid of them, but we stood out against it.'

'Good,' Andrew said. 'One should protect one's heritage.'

'Well, have a nice visit,' the man said.

'Thank you.'

Andrew descended to the pavement and asked a man who was standing there, waiting to get into the tram, if he could direct him to police headquarters.

The man gave him intricate instructions, which made it sound as if the place must be a long way off, yet when Andrew followed them, he found that he reached the block of offices in only a few minutes. Going in, he approached a uniformed constable behind a counter and asked him if it would be possible for him to speak to Detective-Sergeant Ross. There followed so much telephoning, apparently in pursuit of the sergeant, that Andrew felt that his quest was hopeless and that he might as well leave. But eventually the sergeant was tracked down and Andrew was told that if he would sit down, the sergeant would see him shortly. A flicker of hope that Sergeant Ross would not be available and that Andrew would be compelled to abandon his project, like it or not, died as he did so. The course of action to which he had committed himself now seemed to him wildly insane, but there was no escape from it.

Sergeant Ross saw him in a small but pleasantly furnished office with good air-conditioning and a not too formal air. The sergeant himself took Andrew by surprise. He had remembered him as far more heavily built than he was and as looking altogether more formidable than he now appeared. Perhaps it was because of the things that Jan had said about him, but Andrew had believed that the man whom he was coming to see would have a look of bullying strength. Instead he saw a thin, bony man with a high, narrow forehead that had an almost scholarly air, and pale blue eyes which were sombre but not unfriendly. It was only the tilt of his mouth that Andrew had remembered correctly, the way it lifted at one corner, which gave it a permanent sardonic, sceptical smile and which suggested that when he chose he could be formidable.

'I hope I'm not taking up your time for nothing,' Andrew said when they had shaken hands and had both sat down with a wide desk between them. 'But I've got some things on my mind and there's no one else I can think of with whom I can discuss them. I won't pretend, however, that I can tell you anything you're likely to find useful. It's rather the other way round. I'm hoping you can tell me a few things I'd like to know.'

The sergeant raised his eyebrows and the one-sided smile tilted up a little further.

'I'm not much used to answering questions till I get into court,' he said, 'but give it a go.'

'Then I want to ask you,' Andrew said, 'do you seriously believe Mrs Gardiner had anything to do with the murder of her first husband and her sister?'

Sergeant Ross passed a hand across his mouth as if he wanted to blot out his smile and knew no other way of doing it.

'I'm a serious bloke,' he said, 'but I'm not sure if I want to answer that.'

'She thinks you do believe it, you know,' Andrew went on. 'She thinks you've made up your mind she's guilty.'

'Is that right?'

'You know it's right. Haven't you been trying deliberately to keep her frightened?'

'Deliberately, you say. In a case like this you don't do as many things deliberately as you might think. You probe till you suddenly begin to get that feeling in your bones . . . But you aren't interested in that.'

'I'm interested in Mrs Gardiner's alibi,' Andrew said. 'I don't mean for her sister's death. I know she's none for that. But she told me you'd been questioning her only a few days ago about where she was when Luke Wilding was killed.'

The sergeant nodded. 'That's right. We got some new information and I wanted to find out what she had to say about it.'

'Information about a Mrs Mayhew—I think that was the name—who's supposed to have been in the hardware shop in Hartwell when Mrs Gardiner came in to buy some bags for her freezer.'

'You're very well informed,' the sergeant observed.

'Mrs Gardiner told me the story herself just after you'd seen her,' Andrew said. 'She says the man who runs the hardware store, whose name I don't remember—'

'Preston.'

'Yes, Preston. She says he claims she didn't come into the shop until around twelve o'clock, when she says she went in about nine o'clock, after having been dropped there by her husband. If she's telling the truth, of course, it gives her an alibi, because even if she'd driven to the quarry with her husband, she'd have had to walk back, and could hardly have got to Preston's shop almost as soon as it opened.'

'But if she isn't telling the truth and it was twelve o'clock when she and Mrs Mayhew were in the store, she'd have had time to walk back, which puts a different complexion on it, doesn't it?'

'Have you questioned Mrs Mayhew about this?'

The sergeant brought the tips of his fingers together and looked down at them thoughtfully, as if he could not make up his mind whether or not to answer. Then after a little while he looked up at Andrew.

'I can't see why I shouldn't tell you about that,' he said. 'Mrs Mayhew's in Sydney and the Sydney police have asked her a few questions for us. As we've got the story now, Mrs Mayhew was in Preston's store about twelve o'clock on the day of the murder and she did see Mrs Gardiner come in.'

'About twelve o'clock?'

'Yes.'

'So her story that she was there at nine o'clock is untrue?'

'I can't say that. Perhaps she was there at nine *and* at twelve. Her husband might have dropped her there at nine, waited for her, then driven her on with him to the quarry. If that happened, I don't know why she should have gone back to the shop at twelve, but she might have had some reason for doing it. And remember, none of this is on oath. There hasn't even been an inquest. Everyone concerned can change their stories if they feel like it before we get around to anything positive. It's always best to keep that in mind.'

'All the same, I think I know now what you believe,' Andrew said. 'It's possible, if not certain, that Mrs Gardiner could have been on the scene of Luke Wilding's murder, but if she was, she's been covering up for the murderer, and she may be for her sister's murderer too, and I can think of only two reasons why she might do that.'

The sergeant's eyebrows went up again. He waited for Andrew to go on.

'She may be frightened of someone,' Andrew said, 'or she may be shielding someone.'

'Or both. Had you thought of that?'

'I can't say I had, but I agree it's possible.'

'And even if you don't know who may have frightened her, you've probably a fairly clear idea about whom she might shield.'

'Ah,' Andrew said, 'I see. So that's what you think. I've had a feeling all along that that was it.'

'I don't believe I've said I think anything.'

Andrew stood up. 'But I think we understand each other. Well, thank you for giving me your time.'

'My pleasure,' the sergeant replied. 'Nothing else you'd like to ask me while you're about it?'

'As a matter of fact, there's one thing,' Andrew said. 'I've been wondering if it's necessary for me to remain here. I don't think I'm much use to anyone. In fact, I feel rather in the way. Would you have any objection to my moving on?'

'Where are you thinking of going?'

'I'm going to stay with some friends in Sydney in about a fortnight's time, but of course they aren't expecting me yet, so I thought I might pay a visit beforehand to Tasmania.'

'Beautiful country, Tasmania.'

'So I've been told. I've heard it's rather like the Highlands of Scotland, but with a blue sky over it.'

'Sounds about right, though the only time I went there it rained without stopping for three days. But perhaps you'll be luckier than I was. Just leave us your address before you go. Enjoy your trip.'

'Thank you,' Andrew said as he had said to the friendly conductor on the tram.

Making his way out to the street, he was fortunate enough, almost at once, to pick up a taxi.

When he reached the Gardiners' bungalow there were lights in the windows of the living-room, but the rest of the house was in darkness. It had begun to worry him in the taxi that Tony and Jan had probably held back their evening meal until he should return. When, on an impulse, he had set off on the Glenelg tram, he had not thought of that, or that they might have been concerned about what was keeping him out so long. But now, he supposed, he would have to explain himself, though he was not sure how much he wanted to tell. Not the whole of it, that was certain. Perhaps none of it. He might say that he had fallen asleep on the bench. Yet Jan and Tony might have heard the taxi drive up to the gate, which would take a little explaining. The only thing to do, he thought, was to see how the situation developed.

When he rang the doorbell, Tony came to open the door.

'So you got here at last,' he said. 'We thought you must have got lost.'

He did not seem much concerned or curious about it, so Andrew thought he could treat the remark as one that did not need an answer.

'Lovely evening,' he said. 'I met the Nicholls. We had quite a long chat.'

'Well, come in and have a drink. I'll get some food in a minute.'

'I hope you haven't been waiting for me.'

'No, it's only a cold chicken I got from the barbecue place down the road. We've been sitting talking, going round and round what's happened and getting nowhere.'

Tony led the way into the living-room. Sam Ramsden, Denis Lightfoot and Bob Wilding were there, all sprawling in easy chairs with glasses of whisky in their hands. But Jan was not in the room.

Andrew asked where she was.

'She's still lying down,' Tony answered. 'She doesn't want to come out and talk to anyone. I don't think there's anything the matter with her except sheer shock. I suggested we ought to get our doctor round to give her a sedative, but she won't hear of it. She says all she wants is to be left in peace. And that's probably sensible. Now what will you have, Andrew? Whisky?'

'Please.'

Tony poured out a drink and brought it to him and he sat down and sipped the whisky. It was only as he did so that he realized how much he had been wanting it. He looked at Sam Ramsden.

'Staying here for the night, Sam?' he asked.

'Too right, I am,' Sam said. 'I've done enough driving

for one day and there are no planes as late as this.'

'But Denis and I ought not to be staying on like this,' Bob Wilding said, 'getting under Tony's feet and worrying Jan. If we left I dare say she'd come out of hiding.'

'I don't think it would make much difference,' Tony said. 'She doesn't want to talk to me any more than to you.'

There was bitterness in his tone and Andrew noticed that Sam gave him a thoughtful glance.

'She'll get over that,' Sam said. 'Don't worry about it now, Tony. Give her time.'

There was an unusual look of sullen hostility on Tony's face as he glanced at Sam. There was a good deal of hostility in the room, Andrew thought, in spite of the fact that the four men were drinking together, talking quietly and so far as he knew were old friends. Suspicion was making them antagonistic to one another. One of them, so at least three of them thought, was probably a murderer, while the fourth must fear what the suspicions of the others might bring to light.

Looking from face to face, Andrew pondered what he ought to do. Sam, he thought, looked much as he always had since he had first seen him. He looked old, far older than Andrew guessed he was. No doubt the deep wrinkling on his face came from a life spent mostly out of doors in all weathers, but it was more expressionless than Andrew had seen it before. Sam was keeping his thoughts to himself, and they were not pleasant thoughts.

On the other hand, Denis's neat, oval face expressed far more than usual. There was brooding anger on it, not directed at anyone in particular, but somehow at them all and at the room and perhaps most of all at himself. He had the look of a man who has made some fatal mistake which it is now too late to put right and who will never forgive himself for what he has done.

Bob Wilding, in his bony-featured, good-looking way, seemed restless and anxious, wanting to escape from the others there yet unable to make up his mind simply to get up and go away. There was an air of bewilderment about him, as if he found himself having to endure an experience for which nothing in his life had prepared him. It made him look very young, in contrast to Sam's look of tired, experienced old age.

'But you know the real reason she ran away from home, Sam,' Tony said. 'Why can't you tell me about it?'

Sam began to fiddle with his hearing-aid, as if he had not quite heard what Tony had said to him.

Tony went on, 'She told you why she did it, I'm sure of it.'

'How many times do I have to tell you that all she's told me is that when she found Kay's body she panicked,' Sam replied, 'and that from sheer habit, because it's what she's always done since she was a kid, she came to me? You and she haven't been married for so very long. She hasn't got used yet to the idea that you're the person she should turn to when she's in trouble.'

'We've known each other most of our lives,' Tony said.

'That isn't quite the same as being man and wife,' Sam responded.

'But she ought to know she can trust me.'

'I can't help it if she doesn't.'

'I still believe you know the truth, Dad. If you'd tell it me, I might be able to help her.'

Sam shook his head. 'Honest, I don't know any more than I've told you, Tony.'

'I think Sam's right, Tony,' Bob Wilding said. 'Don't worry her. Give her time. That's what I'm trying to do myself—I mean, about Sara. It's not going to help her if I try to rush things. What I've got to do is get her a good lawyer, tell her I'll stand by her whatever she's been doing, and not lose my head. I could have killed Dudley when I heard him talk this afternoon, but that wouldn't have helped anybody.'

'So you're coming round to the idea that Dudley was telling the truth and that Sara's been peddling drugs.' There was contempt in Tony's voice. 'You can't have much faith in her.'

'It isn't a question of having faith,' Bob said. 'If the police have found solid evidence against her, I've got to face that, haven't I? And then I've got to make sure she has the best help I can get her.'

'But you'll still marry her?'

Bob hesitated for a moment before he answered. 'That's something we'll have to talk over when all this is behind us.'

'So you've decided against it already,' Tony said with the same contempt as before.

'Drop it, Tony,' Denis said. 'Bob's quite right, he and Sara can only wait. If it turns out Sara isn't the person he thought she was, I don't see why he shouldn't pull out.'

'Have you been wondering if Kay wasn't the person you thought she was?' Tony asked. 'Was she a blackmailer, for instance?'

A wave of colour swept over Denis's pale face. 'That's a bloody thing to say.'

'But have you?'

Denis did not reply. He swallowed his whisky quickly and stood up.

'Coming, Bob?' he said. 'Tony seems to want to quarrel with someone, but I'm in no mood to indulge him myself. Let's go.'

'Perhaps he had better quarrel with me,' Andrew said.

He had at last made up his mind how to proceed, though the thought of what he intended to do scared him a little. The heads of the other men there turned towards him. He had a feeling that until he had spoken they had almost forgotten his presence in the room. Now they all looked at him with faintly puzzled expressions on their faces. Actually he had not been listening very carefully to what they had been saying, because he had heard something else which had held his attention. It had been the sound of a door opening and closing somewhere in the house and then what he thought was a soft footstep in the kitchen. Then again there was silence. There was no repetition of the opening and closing of the door.

He raised his voice a little, though he knew that he had no need to raise it much because of those years of lecturing in which he had learnt to make it carry without his having to speak noticeably louder. But he spoke directly to the door.

'I think I ought to tell you, Tony,' he said, 'I went into the city to see the police this evening. I had a brief chat with Sergeant Ross.'

'What in hell made you do that?' Tony asked.

'Primarily I wanted to find out if they'd any objections to my leaving Adelaide,' Andrew lied. 'I've been thinking, I'm only in your way here, so it occurred to me I might go for a few days to Tasmania, before going on to Sydney. And they didn't mind my doing that so long as I leave them my address.'

'You went to the police at this hour of the night to ask them if they'd mind if you went to Tasmania?' Tony said. 'I don't believe it, any more than I believe Sam when he says he doesn't know any more than he's told us. What's everyone trying to keep me from me? Why can't anyone tell the truth? Why did you really go, Andrew?'

Andrew was listening carefully. There was still silence in the passage. There had been no recurrence of the soft footfall that he was almost sure he had heard.

'Well, I wanted to check up on something besides,' he said. 'And I found what Ross told me rather disturbing, not only because of what he actually said, but because of what I've deduced from it. I may be quite mistaken, of course, but I think I've a fairly good idea of how his mind is working and I really don't like it.'

Denis appeared to have abandoned the idea of going home and had sat down again.

'I want to hear this,' he said.

Tony gave Andrew a hard stare, the most hostile that he remembered ever having seen on Tony's normally friendly face during all the years of their friendship.

'Go on,' Tony said.

'You see, Tony, I think you're the chief suspect for both murders,' Andrew said. 'And that's what Ross has really been trying to get out of Jan all this time. He's been trying to get her to break down and incriminate you. I don't know if the law here is more or less based on English law, and if it's the same in this kind of case, it would mean that Jan can't give evidence against you, because a wife can't give evidence against her husband. Even if you killed Kay and Jan saw you do it, she couldn't give evidence against you. But you weren't married to her when Luke Wilding was killed, so if Ross can prove that you and she were in the quarry at the time of his murder, he might be able to make out a pretty good case against you, and that's what I think he's wanted to do all along.'

Tony's face had become quite blank. He went on staring at Andrew, but even the hostility was gone from his eyes. Their gaze was merely empty.

'Go on,' he said again in a soft voice.

'To go back to the murder in the quarry, then,' Andrew said, 'the police can prove that Jan lied about her whereabouts that morning. I'm afraid you've got to face it, Tony, Jan is a skilled and determined liar. A certain Mrs Mayhew has stated that she was in the ironmonger's in Hartwell that morning at about twelve o'clock and saw Jan come in then and make some purchases. Jan's said she came in about nine o'clock, having been dropped off there by her husband, and that then she walked home. If she'd done that the only way she could have got to the quarry would have been on foot, in which case she'd have had to walk back as well, and

I believe the distance from the quarry to Hartwell is around ten kilometres, so that would have taken her several hours. I suppose she might have got a lift from someone, but no one's come forward to say so. And if she'd gone with her husband in his car, she'd only have had the walk back to face, and could have got to the shop easily by twelve o'clock.' He hesitated. 'I believe these are facts I'm giving you. The Mayhew woman has been traced and I gather is quite positive about her evidence.'

'I don't understand,' Denis said as Tony stood speechless. 'Why should Jan have said she went into the shop at all? Why shouldn't she have said she stayed at home all the morning?'

'I suppose because she thought the ironmonger would remember she'd been in,' Andrew said, 'but hoped she could confuse him about the time it was.'

'But why should she have gone in at all?' Denis asked.

'That's something you'll have to ask her.'

'This is unbelievable,' Tony muttered. He was no longer looking at Andrew, but down at his hands which were clenched tightly together, as if he were having trouble preventing them from doing something desperate.

'Are you beginning to wonder if Jan isn't the person you thought she was?' Bob asked with a hint of malice in his voice. 'I wonder what you'll do about it.'

'I still don't understand,' Denis said. There was a kind of hopefulness as well as a new interest in his tone. Andrew was not talking about Kay, or about Denis himself. It seemed as if he felt that this should be encouraged. 'Even if Jan did go to the quarry with Luke that morning, we know she didn't murder him. She couldn't have moved the body to the pool. That's been accepted from the first. So there must have been someone else there to do it for her, but why should the police think it was Tony—because that's what you think they do, isn't it?'

'Let's suppose she was there and that it happened like

this,' Andrew said. 'I'm not saying it did, but it's what could have happened. Suppose Jan went to the quarry with her husband that morning. He was what you call a rock-hound and she either shared his interest or simulated it and went with him. What was in her mind when she did we'll never know, unless she tells us. Then something happened while they were there. He found a lump of crystal and perhaps was thinking of making for home with it when she saw her opportunity. She lifted the crystal and brought it down on his skull. And whether that killed him, or whether she had to have help with it is another thing we don't know. But there's something we do know, and that's that someone else was there with her, who moved the body to the pond. And who had the best motive for doing that, if you understand the real reason why it was done?'

'The real reason?' Sam said. 'Wasn't it to get it to the car and drive away and dump it somewhere?'

'It could have been, but it could have been for a quite different reason,' Andrew said. 'I think when you're trying to interpret a puzzling series of events it's as well to ask yourself what the result of them really was. Because there may have been a purpose at the back of them. What was the result of the moving of Luke Wilding's body? Wasn't it the assumption that Jan couldn't have done the murder, or at least done it by herself? It gave her a kind of alibi. I believe that Luke Wilding's body was moved and dumped in the pond simply for that reason. It was done to protect her. And who was as likely to have been there and to have done that as Tony?'

'Now listen,' Sam said, 'your're talking a lot of shit. Why was it likely to have been Tony? Granted he may have seen things were crook in the marriage and sometimes felt like killing Wilding. I did myself. But I know he knew Jan was planning to leave Luke, because I told him that myself.'

'But didn't that make the murder essential for him?' Andrew said. 'If Jan had left Wilding, he'd have changed his will pretty soon and she wouldn't have inherited his money. And wasn't it simply to get hold of it that she married him? She told me herself she'd been in love with Tony for a long time, but that he hadn't seemed to realize she existed until after she married Wilding. And perhaps he didn't. Perhaps it took her becoming a potentially rich woman to make an impression on him. On the other hand, perhaps they had it worked out together from the start. Perhaps Wilding was doomed from the day he married her.'

Tony lifted his head slowly and gazed at Andrew with an expression of dazed horror.

'My God, and I thought we were friends,' he said. 'But go on. Say the rest of it.'

'I don't think there's much else to say.'

'Aren't you forgetting that I must have killed Kay yesterday afternoon?'

'Yes,' Denis said, 'that's difficult to believe. Why did Tony do it?'

'I should have thought that was obvious enough,' Andrew said.

He had noticed the uncomfortable beating of his heart again as tension in the room mounted and as apprehension began to fill his mind. He had gambled and was beginning to feel extremely afraid that the gamble was not going to pay off.

'Didn't Jan tell Kay everything?' he said. 'Haven't we been told that a number of times? D'you think she didn't tell Kay the truth about what happened in the quarry? But at that time she didn't know something about Kay which we've only learnt today from Dudley Blair. Kay wasn't above a touch of blackmail. Of course Sara Massingham's connection with drugs and Luke Wilding's murder in themselves had nothing to do with each other. The only thing they had in common was that each provided Kay with a victim. She knew the truth about them both through her sister, and the power that they gave her over Sara as well as Tony may have led to her death. If she'd been making Tony pay her blackmail and he'd got tired of it and he'd found out that Sara was another victim, he may have thought it was a good time to get rid of Kay and hope her knowledge of Sara's drug-peddling would be taken as a motive for her murder. And Jan drove straight off to her father after it because she didn't trust herself to talk to us down on the beach without giving away that she knew what had happened. And Tony draped his head and shoulders in the green towel and slipped down to the beach and dropped it there and swam out to sea, quite inconspicuous in the crowds there were on the beach that afternoon—'

The door suddenly swung open. Jan was standing there in the passage, wearing a dressing-gown and with her feet bare. Her enormous eyes shone with a terrible lustre in her small, pale face.

'It's all a lie!' she shrieked. 'Every word of it is an unspeakable lie! Tony had nothing to do with it!'

Andrew let his breath out in a long sigh. At last he could stop his frantic search for more and more words and sit back and relax. The gamble was going to pay off after all.

'Then why don't you come in and tell us the truth, Jan?' he said. 'It's time for that, isn't it?'

CHAPTER 8

Jan advanced into the room, looking at Andrew with fury.

'You did that on purpose,' she said. 'You knew I was there, listening.'

'I thought it was possible,' he admitted.

'And you knew I wouldn't let Tony be suspected.'

'I hoped you wouldn't.'

'And you knew the whole thing was a lie.' Her high-pitched voice trembled.

'It wasn't a lie that the police suspect Tony,' Andrew said. 'It was to find out about that that I went to see them this evening. And Sergeant Ross let on to me he's sure you were on the scene of the crime and that you knew what happened and are shielding somebody. And it's obvious he thinks there's only one person you'd shield. Once I was sure of that, it was easy to reconstruct how he was looking at the whole affair.'

'But why couldn't you keep it to yourself?' she asked. 'Why did you have to try to trap me?'

'Go easy, love,' Sam Ramsden said. 'We all know you've been hiding something. I think Andrew's right, it's time you told the truth about it.'

Tony put an arm round her and drew her to him. 'Yes,' he said. 'Go on.'

'If I were you, I'd be careful what I'd say,' Bob Wilding said. 'If it comes out you've known the truth all along about my father's murder and kept it to yourself, you may find yourself in serious trouble.'

She rested her head on Tony's shoulder.

'Be quiet,' she said, but in an absent tone as if what Bob had said had merely distracted her from what she was trying to think out for herself. 'I haven't been shielding anybody. I mean, not because I wanted to. It's just that I haven't known what to do.'

'Did you see Kay killed?' Denis asked, sounding incredulous.

She lifted her head and nodded. 'Yes.'

'You actually saw it done?'

'Yes, and I screamed. I screamed and screamed, but nobody came. They were all down on the beach.'

'Then I agree with Bob, be careful what you say, even to us,' Denis said. 'This is the sort of situation where the police would say to you, remember that what you say may be taken down and used in evidence against you.'

'That isn't quite what the police actually say,' Tony said.

156

He gently stroked Jan's hair. 'And we aren't the police. Go on, Jan.'

'I'd be careful, Jan,' Bob Wilding said again. 'You may regret what you say.'

'No, Bob, I'm going to tell the truth,' she said, 'and if I were you I'd go before anyone thinks of stopping you.' She looked back at Andrew. 'You knew it was Bob, didn't you?'

'I thought there was some evidence to support that view,' he answered.

Bob sprang to his feet. 'It's a lie. You all know what a liar she is. She's only trying to cover up for Tony. The police are right about him. I've known it from the first and I kept quiet about it only because I'd some sympathy with him. My father was a beast. His violence made my childhood a nightmare, and he was doing the same thing to Jan, once he'd got her in his power. And of course that sickened Tony, because, as anyone could see, he'd been in love with her all along. I don't believe my father's money ever came into his mind. I believe it was his bestial cruelty to Jan that settled things. But even if I was ready not to talk about what I knew, I'm not going to be made a scapegoat for anyone.'

Tony look at Bob sombrely. 'Why don't you let Jan tell her own story?' he said.

'Because it'll only be lies.'

Jan spoke again to Andrew. 'What made you think it was Bob?'

'Kay's murder,' he answered. 'You'd told Kay the truth about what had happened to your husband, hadn't you? And she said she and Bob were together at the time of his death. If that was true, it didn't mean anything, but if by chance it wasn't true, if she was supplying him with a fake alibi, then it gave her a great deal of power over him. And from what she did to Miss Massingham, we know she wasn't above blackmail. I believe as long as she only pressed Wilding for odds and ends of money because of what she'd done for him he paid up without minding too much. But when she put the pressure on Sara Massingham after she found out about her dealings in drugs, she was going too far. Bob decided to put an end to it. And he didn't mind that you were in the house to see what he did because he felt secure that you'd never tell the truth about his father's murder.'

Sam stood up. He put a hand on Bob's shoulder.

'Jan hasn't told her story yet,' he said. 'If I were you, I'd take her advice and go. Nobody here is going to stop you.'

Denis made a small, convulsive movement as if he were about to leap up from his chair and contradict this, but then he sank back.

Bob stood still, looking round from face to face in the room. Then suddenly, as if he thought that someone would try to stop him, he leapt towards the door. He was gone in a moment. They heard the front door slam behind him, then running feet on the gravel outside.

Jan began to shake all over. She turned and hid her face against Tony's chest. Then as if something that had dammed up feeling in her had broken, she began crying violently, clutching at him with both hands. He leant his cheek against her hair, holding her gently.

'There's no hurry now,' he said. 'It can wait.'

'No,' she said between her sobs, 'I want to get it over.'

'Then come and sit down here,' he said, guiding her towards the sofa. 'Shall I get you a drink?'

'No, not now,' she answered. 'Later.'

He sat down beside her. 'I'm glad it's come to this at last. There was always something between us, but we ought to be able to deal with it now.'

She found a handkerchief and mopped her eyes. They were red, her face was blotchy from all the crying that she had done that day and her lips were trembling, but after a moment she drew a deep breath and said, 'I don't know where to start.'

'The beginning is the usual place,' Tony said.

'But what was the beginning? I suppose it was when I made the awful mistake of marrying Luke. He was handsome and he seemed so distinguished and kind. And sometimes he really was like that, except when his bad moods took him. But I needn't go back to all that, or talk about the shock it was to find out what he could really be like. It didn't take me long to make up my mind to leave him. I suppose, considering the kind of man he was, it would have been best just to do it, then write or telephone to say I wasn't coming back. But I'd got it into my head the honest thing would be to tell him to his face what I was going to do, and I'd made up my mind I'd do it that morning in the quarry. He wanted me to go with him and I drove there with him in the Mercedes. I didn't go into Preston's shop at nine o'clock. Saying I did was just a muddled sort of attempt to give myself an alibi. I guessed he'd remember I'd been in that morning, but I thought there was a good chance he wouldn't remember when. Luke and I went straight to the quarry, and then Luke got to work on a rock where he was sure there was a geode, and sure enough, in only a little while he found it and found a wonderful lump of crystal. And of all stupid times to choose, just when he was feeling on top of the world, that was when I began to tell him I was going to leave him.'

Her voice had grown steadier, but at that point she gave another shiver.

'I might have known what he'd do,' she said. 'He struck me. I nearly fell off the ledge we were on and I suddenly became terrified that he was going to kill me. I saw him reaching for the pickaxe he'd been using. I wish I could say I don't remember what happened next, but I remember it horribly clearly. I picked up the lump of crystal and I hit him with it. He fell down. There was blood on his forehead where I'd hit him, but he started cursing, so I knew I hadn't killed him. I dropped the crystal and I was just going to run away when suddenly, appearing out of nowhere, that was how it seemed, Bob was there and had the crystal in his hand and was battering Luke's head with it. Then I remember Bob gave a queer kind of laugh and said, "Who's going to know you didn't do that?"' She paused and said to Tony in a tone that had suddenly become oddly childish, 'I'd like that whisky now. And a cigarette. My cigarettes are in the bedroom.'

He got up and went to fetch them. While he was gone she sat with her elbows on her knees and her face hidden in her hands. Returning, he lighted a cigarette for her, then poured out some whisky. She drew hungrily on the cigarette, but at first looked at the glass in her hand as if she could not think how it had got there. But then she sipped a little from it, then a little more and when she spoke again the childish note in her voice, which had threatened hysteria, had gone.

'Just at first, you know, it didn't seem strange to me that Bob was there. And another queer thing was that I felt as if it had really been I who had killed Luke. Then I did ask Bob why he'd come to the quarry and he told me with another frightening sort of laugh that he'd been waiting a long time for the right time and place. He said he'd known where Luke and I would be, because his father had telephoned him in Adelaide that morning and had mentioned where we were going. So then I began to understand that he hadn't killed Luke just to protect me, as I thought at first, but that he'd come there on purpose to do it. I realized there was the same sort of violence in him that there was in Luke, only even worse, and I began to be horribly frightened. Then he said to me, "Of course, if you like, we can fix that. I can give you an alibi if you'll get one for me." I didn't understand what he meant, but he explained that if he dragged Luke's body down to the pond and left it there, no one could ever think I'd been able to do it, but in return he wanted me to say we'd been together at home, or something like that.'

'Why didn't you do that?' Denis asked. 'Why did you bring Kay into it?'

'It was Bob's idea. When he'd thought it over he said there wasn't much point in our saying we'd been together, because we were the two people who'd benefit by Luke's death, each of us inheriting a good deal under his will, so it was going to look suspicious if we said we'd been together. So I said, "I'll fix it with Kay." He and she were seeing a lot of each other at that time, in fact people thought they were probably going to get married, so if they said they'd been out together it wouldn't seem unlikely to anyone. And I knew she'd do what I asked when I told her what had happened. So Bob drove me back to Hartwell and dropped me off just before we got there, and I went into the town to get to a public telephone and call Kay to say, if she was asked, that she and Bob had set out together an hour or so earlier. It never occurred to me she'd use that against him when it suited her. I'd rather depended on her all my life and trusted her completely.'

'But why did you go into Preston's shop?' Sam asked. 'You must have known you were risking drawing attention to yourself just when you didn't want it.'

'I did it because I saw you coming,' she said.

'You saw *me*!' Sam exclaimed.

'Yes, the phone's just outside Preston's shop,' Jan said, 'and I was just going to it when I saw you, and I knew if you saw me you'd stop and talk and probably insist on driving me home, and there was so little time to spare. Bob would be picking Kay up in only a little while and I wanted to speak to her and ask her to do just what Bob said without any arguing. Of course there wasn't time for me to go home to make the call. But just as I was going to do it I saw you coming, and I dodged into Preston's shop so that you shouldn't see me. I didn't think for a moment he'd remember my coming in, and anyway he's such a muddled old fool I felt sure my word would be accepted rather than his if I stuck to it that I'd been in the shop much earlier in the morning than he said. And so it was officially until Mrs Mayhew turned up with her evidence, though I know Sergeant Ross never believed me.'

'And so Kay agreed to help you,' Denis said bitterly. 'But then she decided it would suit her better to blackmail a murderer than to marry him. And so she married me. That's how it happened, isn't it, Jan?'

'I suppose it was, Denis,' she agreed.

'And she never cared much for either of us.'

Sam spoke brusquely, 'Kay never cared for anyone in her life but herself. You'll get over it, Denis, when you get used to thinking of her as the person she really was.'

'But that's the problem, isn't it?' Denis said. His neat, self-contained face looked blank and lifeless, as if something in him had died. 'To have your whole world stood on its head in twenty-four hours or so. Because I loved the woman, you know. She was lovely. She was gay. She was everything to me. And now I've somehow got to get accustomed to the idea that she wasn't worth it. But why did she have to be killed, Jan? I don't understand that.'

'As Andrew said, because she started to blackmail Sara,' Jan answered. 'I don't believe she did it for the money. It was for the sweet sense of power. But Bob's really in love with Sara and he was ready to do anything she told him. And that meant what her brother wanted. So Bob came back to the house when you were all down on the beach and for all I know, all he meant to do was argue with her and tell her she'd got to lay off Sara. But Kay laughed at him and that was a dangerous thing to do with Bob, just as it was with Luke. I was in the bedroom at the time, changing, so I didn't see how it actually happened, but I heard the laugh turn into a scream and I came running out and there was Bob standing over Kay and battering her head in with that lump of crystal, just as he did when he killed Luke. And that's when I began to scream myself and he dropped the crystal and put his hand over my mouth and told me to be quiet, or he could still get me convicted for Luke's death, and now Kay's as well. Nobody knew I hadn't been alone with her in the house, he said. I couldn't think properly and I believed him, so all I wanted was to get away. But I didn't think of joining the rest of you because I thought if I told you what had happened it would only drive Bob into saying he'd found Luke dead already when he arrived in the quarry and that everything I'd said about that was a lie. And I knew I wasn't capable of joining you and pretending I hadn't seen anything. So that's why I ran away home and got the Volvo and drove up to Dad. It seemed the natural thing to do. But I didn't tell him any of this. I only told him that I'd found Kay dead and didn't know who'd done it.'

'So we've let the murderer escape,' Tony said. 'Perhaps that wasn't very clever of us.'

Andrew did not feel sure of that. He thought of what might have happened there if they had not let Bob Wilding go. A nasty scene, at the very least. But he wondered what they were going to do about Jan, because like it or not, she had concealed evidence against two crimes. That was a serious offence, though perhaps the fact that she had been intimidated might help her.

She leant her head against Tony's shoulder. She looked relaxed, with an air almost of contentment about her.

'I think I want to tell the whole thing to the police,' she said. 'I don't think I can live with secrets any longer. I'm not naturally a liar, you know. It's felt worse and worse as time went by. I don't think I could have borne it much longer. And if we were all to keep all this to ourselves, one day that man Ross would pounce on Tony and then I'd have to tell the truth anyway.' She turned to Andrew. 'I suppose he gave you a hint that that was what he was going to do and you followed it up, as he wanted you to.'

'That was more or less how it was,' he admitted, 'though we didn't actually discuss it.'

'I don't know what will happen to me when I tell them the truth,' she said, 'but at least some day I'll be clear of it all, instead of living all the time with a deadly fear at the back of my mind.' She picked up one of Tony's hands and held it against her cheek. 'Our marriage hasn't been much good to you, has it, Tony darling? You must have been very unhappy.'

'Not unhappy,' he answered. 'Just worried, puzzled, wondering when our difficulties would solve themselves. But sure that they would in the end.'

'Where d' you think Bob's gone?' Sam asked abruptly.

Nobody answered. There was silence for a time.

Then Denis observed, 'He must have known that once Jan decided to talk in front of all of us here, there was no way out for him.'

'But what does a person do when there's no way out?' Sam went on.

'Depends on the person,' Tony said.

Andrew wondered what he himself would do if he found himself in a situation from which there was no way out. Shoot himself, perhaps, if he had a gun? Poison himself, if the right sort of pills were available? Swim out to sea till he met a shark? Or perhaps just present himself at police headquarters and make a confession?

The truth was, he thought that the last was by far the most likely course for him to pursue. Shrinking in revulsion from violence in all its forms, he knew that that would include violence against himself. But then, feeling as he did, he recognized that it was next door to impossible that he should ever find himself in Bob Wilding's situation, with two murders to his credit.

'Well, what are you going to do, love?' Sam asked after a pause. 'I don't think there's anyone in this room who won't keep quiet, if that's what you want.'

Jan shook her head. 'No, I told you, I want to tell the truth. But I'm not sure how to go about it. Tony, perhaps you would drive me in to police headquarters.'

'What, right away?' he said, recoiling sharply.

'Yes, I think so,' she answered. 'Yes, please, right away.'

Andrew saw Sergeant Ross once more before he left for Tasmania, and that was by chance.

By then Jan had been remanded on bail and was at home, waiting for the inquest into Luke Wilding's death, the date of which had at last been fixed, and into that of her sister. From the time of Jan's return home from a brief spell of custody there had been a change in the atmosphere of the Gardiner household which had made Andrew certain that it was time for him to leave. Tony, as before, had pressed him to stay on, but this time Andrew had resisted and he had felt fairly sure that in fact this was greeted by relief. Tony and Jan were in the process of forging a new relationship and however hospitable their instincts might be, it seemed clear to Andrew that they would be better able to do this without an audience.

He was glad to see what seemed to be happening to them. The tension between them that had disturbed him, the barrier of distrust that had seemed to him to be there in spite of their obvious love for one another, was gone. They clung to one another in a new way, peaceful in spite of the uncertainty of the future.

So it was time for him, Andrew thought, to be moving on.

However, before he left he had a day with the Nicholls. They had invited him to go for a picnic with them to one of the nature reserves near the city. It occurred to him, when they suggested this, that on this visit he had not seen a single kangaroo, which seemed a pity, and in accepting their invitation he hoped that he would see one or two, bounding about in the scrub.

165

In fact, he saw a tribe of them, as interested in studying him, it appeared, as he was in observing them. He wished that he had thought of bringing a camera with him, though he had never been much of a photographer. David, however, had one, and went as close to the animals as they would permit to take several pictures of them and promising Andrew that he would send him prints once he knew that Andrew had reached home.

They had settled for their picnic on the shore of a lake where there were a few tables and benches in the shade of some tall gums. There were pelicans on the lake, sailing along with almost the majesty of swans and when Andrew and the Nicholls had sat down at one of the tables and Clare had unpacked the picnic basket that she and David had brought with them, some small, pretty, pale brown birds came round their feet, hoping for crumbs. They were beguilingly free of all fear of humans. The water was a dull, greenish colour with some pale, dead skeletons of trees along its brink, killed by a change in its level.

Clare had provided a meal of crayfish and salad, some chicken sandwiches, then raspberries and cream. They drank two bottles of a dry white wine and ended up with coffee from a Thermos. For some days Andrew had hardly given a thought to the fact that this was the end of December and that there was anything strange about raspberries being in season. But it happened that the day of the picnic was New Year's Day and for once, forgetting murder, forgetting guilt, forgetting fear, he let himself think of the other things that he had forgotten during the last week or two, the biting winds of home, the leaden skies, the probable sleet or snow. He was just allowing himself to take great pleasure in the sunshine, the still water and the chirruping birds, when he saw Sergeant Ross advancing towards him.

But this was an unfamiliar Sergeant Ross. He was in shorts and a shirt of flaming pink and he was carrying a two-year-old child in his arms. Another child, perhaps two years older, followed close on his heels, and a slim, pretty woman in a gaily flowered dress brought up the rear of the party. Plainly it was Sergeant Ross's day off.

He had almost reached the table at which Andrew and the Nicholls were seated before he noticed them. When he did so, he gave no sign of having recognized them, but either out of tact, or because he did not want his professional life to intrude into his private, he turned his back on them and quietly steered his family towards a table some distance away.

David gave a grin.

'Nice-looking kids,' he remarked. 'And a nice shirt.' His gaze followed the sergeant's blaze of pink.

'Lairy,' Clare said.

It was the first Australian word that was completely foreign to Andrew.

His incomprehension must have shown on his face, for David said, 'You don't know what that means, Andrew? It means the same as gaudy, flashy, and it's the last thing I'd ever have dreamt our sergeant would have a taste for. But then I've never asked myself what does a detective do when he isn't detecting.'

'Poor man,' Clare said. 'Rough on him to come across us when he's got a holiday. I wonder what he and his wife are talking about. I don't suppose it would be murder in front of the children.'

'I wonder if he feels left high and dry, now that Luke Wilding's murder's solved,' David said. 'If he does, being an Australian, he'll think about cricket. Or the next murder on the books.'

Andrew remembered that on the day of his arrival Tony had told him that besides being called the City of Churches, Adelaide was famous for the bizarre crimes that had happened there. It struck him that if that was true Sergeant Ross's life was unlikely ever to be short of interest.

He was thinking about this a few days later when the

plane for Melbourne, where he would have to change to reach Tasmania, lifted from the ground and as it left the airport swung out over the sea. Looking down from it, he had a brief glimpse of the narrow strip of sand along the beach, the guardian pines and the neat-looking bungalows, all rapidly disappearing as the plane climbed. Tony had promised that he would write to tell him the end of the story, but Andrew could not help feeling that in Tony's place he probably would not do so. Bizarre crimes may be very interesting when they happen to other people, but to someone involved in one they can only mean pain.

Yet in the end, a few weeks after Andrew had left his friends in Sydney, a letter came from Tony. Jan, he wrote, had not yet had to face her trial and did not know what was likely to happen to her, but they had found a very smart lawyer who thought he might get her off altogether, and she was calmer and happier than she had been for a long time. Sara Massingham had been sentenced to two years in prison. The Honourable Dudley Blair, as his habit had always been, had vanished without a trace into the outback. Clare and David Nicholl were expecting their first child. Denis Lightfoot was already showing signs of taking a marked interest in a lively Irishwoman who was acting as his housekeeper. Sam Ramsden had returned to his solitude among his vines and olives and did not welcome visitors. And nothing had ever been seen or heard of Bob Wilding but a pair of shoes, which probably belonged to him and which had been found on the beach at Betty Hill. Tony wrote that he left Andrew to draw his own conclusions.

What Andrew concluded was that Bob, giving up all hope of escaping the consequences of his actions, had either swum out to sea till he tired and drowned, or else perhaps had met with a shark. But Tony did not mention whether or not the shark-patrol, still busy advertising rum, had spotted one and sounded a siren. It should not be forgotten, Andrew thought, that Australia is a very large country in which it should not be too difficult to disappear, that Bob might have left his shoes where he had simply so that it should be assumed he had met his end in the sea, but that in fact the sharks had gone hungry.